JUMP

ELISA CARBONE

VIKING
An Imprint of Penguin Group (USA) Inc.

VIKING
Published by Penguin Group
Penguin Group (USA) Inc., 345 Hudson Street, New York, New York 10014, U.S.A.
Penguin Group (Canada), 90 Eglinton Avenue East, Suite 700, Toronto, Ontario, Canada M4P 2Y3
(a division of Pearson Penguin Canada Inc.)
Penguin Books Ltd, 80 Strand, London WC2R 0RL, England
Penguin Ireland, 25 St Stephen's Green, Dublin 2, Ireland (a division of Penguin Books Ltd)
Penguin Group (Australia), 250 Camberwell Road, Camberwell, Victoria 3124, Australia
(a division of Pearson Australia Group Pty Ltd)
Penguin Books India Pvt Ltd, 11 Community Centre, Panchsheel Park, New Delhi – 110 017, India
Penguin Group (NZ), 67 Apollo Drive, Rosedale, North Shore 0632, New Zealand
(a division of Pearson New Zealand Ltd.)
Penguin Books (South Africa) (Pty) Ltd, 24 Sturdee Avenue, Rosebank,
Johannesburg 2196, South Africa

Penguin Books Ltd, Registered Offices: 80 Strand, London WC2R 0RL, England

First published in 2010 by Viking, a member of Penguin Group (USA) Inc.

1   3   5   7   9   10   8   6   4   2

Copyright © Elisa Carbone, 2010
All rights reserved

LIBRARY OF CONGRESS CATALOGING-IN-PUBLICATION DATA
Carbone, Elisa Lynn.
Jump / by Elisa Carbone.
p. cm.
Summary: Two teenaged runaways meet at a climbing gym and together
embark on a dangerous and revealing journey.
ISBN 978-0-670-01185-8 (hardcover)
[1. Runaways—Fiction. 2. Rock climbing—Fiction. 3. Interpersonal relations—Fiction.] I. Title.
PZ7.C1865Ju 2010
[Fic]—dc22
2009030175

Printed in U.S.A.
Set in Melior
Book design by Kate Renner

For Jim
my partner in the adventure

ONE

CRITTER

Things I know to be true:

1. I am not my body.
2. I am part of a force so huge and powerful, it defies understanding.
3. I am that force.
4. The things I see and touch—the wall, the window, my fingers spread in front of the sunlight, my hair falling into my eyes—are no more solid than the air. It is all illusion.
5. There is absolutely nothing to be afraid of.
6. According to my parents and the doctors here, I am insane.

TWO

P. K.

I. Will. Not. Give. In.

Boarding school—my parents' latest idea in a long line of "remedies" they think will fix me. As if I need to be fixed, like a broken ice maker that suddenly refuses to make perfectly shaped ice cubes, identical to all the other ice cubes made by all the kids in high school who attend class, care about grades, suck up to teachers, etc.

"It'll be nice, P.K., up in the mountains, away from the city." (Read: away from your friends with the colorful tattoos and hair that smells like incense and God knows what else.)

I should have said, "Daddy might as well take the tuition money and shove it. I'm not going."

Not really. I wouldn't say that.

But actually, it would be a safer thing to do with the tuition money than sending it to that school, buying three plane tickets, packing up enough socks and underwear to last me a month, and dropping me off in the care of some dorm RA and a bunch of teachers determined to cram piles of information into my brain. Boarding school—a jail for the mind. Twenty-four-hour training in how *not* to think for yourself. And starting in June with summer school, no less. As if normal high school wasn't bad enough.

I can just see them leaving, waving good-bye to their little girl at the nice new school they believe will change her into a good student.

Within an hour of them dropping me off, I'll have my backpack stuffed with a few clothes and my climbing gear, and be on the road with my thumb out.

THREE

CRITTER

Service elevator.

It's sort of the Underground Railroad of the psych ward.

I've been able to get at least some of the drugs out of my system. Would have been easier if they hadn't busted me the first time I tried skipping doses, and assigned Nurse Ratshit (I just like to call her that—her real name is Miranda) to stand over me while I swallow, and then check under my tongue. As if Gum Chewing in School 101 didn't teach every kid early on how to hide stuff in their cheeks.

Anyway, I've gotten enough of the drugs cleared out that I've started seeing reality again. I can see the space between the molecules, how things are not solid but made of dancing, swirling light. And I can see the colors of the energy around people's bodies again, too. Miranda is pink-lavender when she falls asleep in her I'm-watching-every-single-one-of-you chair. (She pretends to be reading, but I can tell she's sleeping because of her colors.) And she's mustard-yellow when she's awake and in full Nurse Ratshit mode. I once saw her turn into boiling slate-gray/black when a couple of hospital supervisors came through the ward. Man, I never knew she could get so scared.

It's good to feel more like myself again. I'll need my wits about me when I make my break on the service elevator while Nurse Ratshit is dreaming her pink and lavender dreams.

FOUR

P.K.

Ways to thwart parental domination:

> Age 2—Throw tantrum
> Age 8—Cry and beg, using reasoned arguments
> Age 12—Lock self in bedroom, refuse to talk
> Age 16—Run away

They have brought this upon themselves.

And really, this is a financial decision. If I leave sooner rather than later I'll save them a boatload of money: tuition and plane tickets, not to mention numerous sock, underpants, and bra purchases. I'll see which of my friends wants to go with me, and we can head straight for Eldo.

FIVE

"Although compulsory schooling was begun in this country mainly in hopes of educating people worthy of democracy, other goals also imbedded themselves in the educational system. One was the goal of creating obedient factory workers who did not waste time by talking to each other or daydreaming."

The Teenage Liberation Handbook
by Grace Llewellyn

SIX

CRITTER

1:05 a.m. Nurse Ratshit snoring.

1:10 a.m. Stealthy mental patient sneaks down hallway to service elevator. Adopts "sack of dirty laundry" look by closing self in laundry bag (borrowed for this purpose several days ago and hidden under mattress of hospital bed).

Fear level: zero. (There is never anything to be afraid of, ever. Life is 100 percent adventure.)

Contents of pockets: toothbrush; sunglasses; deodorant; extra T-shirt; recent letter from little sister, Jenna, age thirteen, which states emphatically, "I don't think you're crazy, Critter. I love you." Also, one hundred-dollar bill sent in letter from savvy little sister, which mental patient has had to keep rolled up and hidden in ponytail in order to avoid confiscation.

1:15 a.m. Tired mental patient falls asleep doing excellent "sack of dirty laundry" imitation, while waiting for early morning when mop guy will come with key to make elevator move, hopefully before Nurse Ratshit wakes up and turns mustard yellow, or any manner of angry colors.

SEVEN

P.K.

The best reception for my cell phone is up in the tree house my brothers Les and Tom built when they were kids. This works well, because it makes for private conversations. In the dark my cell phone screen glows. I press the number two and my best friend's number dials. Not that I think Daria will actually go with me. Why should she? She was as miserable in school as I am, but she showed her mom and dad *The Teen-age Liberation Handbook* and they *got* it. Now she spends her days reading; working through biology, chemistry, and math textbooks at her own pace so she'll be on track to get into preveterinary medicine in college; volunteering at the local animal shelter; and, of course, hanging with me and the rest of our friends.

"Hi, P.K."

"Hi, Daria. You want to come to Eldo with me?"

"Oh my God, your parents are letting you plan a trip to Eldorado Canyon? That's *awesome*! Who else is going? When are you leaving?"

I pick her last question to answer first. "I'm leaving day after tomorrow."

"Why didn't you tell me sooner?" she wails. "That's not enough time to talk my parents into letting me go."

I can't stand to hear the hurt in her voice, and I realize I've gone about this all wrong. "Daria, listen. My parents don't exactly know I'm going. It's an emergency trip. It's the best way I can think of to deal with the boarding-school issue."

She is silent and I hear sniffling.

"I just didn't want to leave without inviting you along, you know?" And I know she knows all the unspoken stuff I'm feeling, including how much I wish it could be different.

"What if my mom and dad try to talk to your parents again?" she asks.

I rub my forehead, remembering last year when her parents came over to my house, her mom in a long India-print skirt and her dad in a T-shirt with a picture of the universe and an arrow pointing to somewhere near the center with the words YOU ARE HERE. I don't know if my parents heard anything her parents said about real education and trusting your child's inborn curiosity and how unschooled kids get into college just fine. All my dad could talk about after they left was how irresponsible Daria's parents were for taking her out of school, and what a waste it was of Daria's wonderful ambition to be a veterinarian. He even called the county truancy office, thinking he could force them to put Daria back into school. He was surprised to find out that what they were doing was perfectly legal. But that still didn't open his mind toward any freedom for his own daughter.

"No," I say softly. "It won't help, but thanks." Suddenly I don't want to talk anymore. "See you at the gym tomorrow?" I ask, my finger itching to push the End button and stop causing Daria pain, or stop hearing the pain I am causing her.

"Yeah—you'll definitely be there?" I hear the fear in her voice, that I might slip away before she sees me again. Fridays at the rock gym have been a standing tradition for over a year now.

"I'll *definitely* be there," I assure her. "I'm going to ask Adam and Pinebox and Slink—see if one of them will go with me to Eldo."

Daria catches her breath. "P.K., you *can't* go alone. Promise me. Even if you fly into Denver, you'll have to hitch a ride up to Eldorado Canyon. Swear you won't go alone." Her voice is strong. "*Swear* it."

I hesitate. There's no guarantee one of the guys will go with me. I'd rather go *with* a climbing partner, but I'll pick up a partner at the Canyon if I have to. Still, I'm planning to hitch the whole way and I don't like the idea of amphetamine-popping, sex-crazed truckers as my only escorts. "All right," I say. "I swear I won't go alone."

I'll adopt a dog from the shelter and take him with me if I have to.

EIGHT

CRITTER

Works like a charm.

Well, except for the part where Nurse Ratshit discovers that the pile of clothes under the covers in my bed is *not* me. The part where she gets on the intercom and alerts everyone that I might be "attempting to leave the premises" is definitely not part of the plan, but I am brilliant in my ability to go with the flow and quickly develop a new strategy. My "pop out of the laundry bag and run like hell, knocking people out of the way" maneuver works very well, and I don't even seriously hurt anyone. I take the "emergency exit only, alarm will sound" stairs two at a time (alarm very loud, but everyone in my ward already awakened by commotion anyway) and crash out into the night, across the parking lots, into the woods beyond, into the quiet, the spaciousness and stillness of dark trees standing in silhouette against a sky with stars winking at me. I take a deep breath, notice my body disappearing in the magnitude of the presence of the stars, sky, trees, and wind. I start walking (body actually still in existence) and join groggy thank-God-it's-Friday commuters on an early-morning bus, bound I know not where, but at least I get on for free because the bus driver does not have change for a one-hundred-dollar bill.

NINE

P. K.

I don't even pretend to go to school and, strangely, my mother says nothing about it. I wander downstairs at noon in my pajamas, looking for food.

"Oh dear," my mother says, eyeing the shredded sleeves of my pajama top. It's my favorite pair, worn to that wonderful just-before-disintegration softness. "We'll need to get you new pj's as well," she says. "You can't wear those in a dormitory around other people."

Can't even take my favorite pajamas with me?! I am about to object when I remember I'm not going anyway, so it's a moot point. I nod and pour myself a bowl of cereal. Might as well be agreeable and give her one more day of peace before I totally freak her out.

I spend the early afternoon in my room organizing my gear, trying to figure out what I can reasonably carry: trad gear, rope, sleeping bag, tent, camp stove . . . it sure would be helpful to have somebody come with me. I wonder how much weight a dog can carry.

At three o'clock I throw my rock shoes, harness, belay device, and chalk bag into my small pack and head downstairs.

"I'm going to the rock gym," I tell my mother, who is typing away at the computer—probably e-mailing one or the other of my brothers, who are both away at college.

"All right, honey," Mom says. "Just don't be back late."

"Not a problem," I say pleasantly. I trot out the door, hop on my bike, and go off in search of a Sherpa.

TEN

CRITTER

A small puddle of drool on my shirt is evidence that I have fallen asleep on the bus. I wonder how many times a bus driver will take you around the city before he kicks you out. Obviously, more than several hours' worth, because when I open my eyes the sun is high and the people on the streets have that "must purchase fast food, cram it into my mouth, and get right back to work/school/criminal activity" kind of look. I hope that as more of the drugs leave my body I won't have to sleep so much.

The bus makes a turn into an area where there are mostly warehouses, and suddenly I see a place I recognize. It's as if my whole self recognizes it and remembers, and I can hardly wait to get off the bus and run over there.

The memories: walking in with Dad and him saying, "You go first," and the feel of fake rock in my hands. Then Dad cheering me on, and me grinning as I slap the biners at the top of a climb.

I pull the cord to ring the bus bell, and the driver lets me out.

ELEVEN

P.K.

"Braille it, man!"

Slink has his feet on microholds, his butt out, his cheek pressed up against the wall, and he's flailing around with his right arm above his head, searching for a hold that will release him from this predicament.

"Slink, if you stick your butt in and stand up like a normal person, you'll be able to *see* the holds," I say sort of helpfully.

He tries my suggestion and falls. Pinebox locks off the belay, and Slink dangles, massaging his forearms.

"It's a five-twelve, you know," Adam says. Adam, who is six feet four with zero body fat. "Let me show you how it's done."

Slink glares at him. "I'm not finished," he shoots down. But he hesitates too long, and we start up the wolflike howling that signifies he is hangdogging.

Slink grabs a couple of holds, tries to rambo his way up the wall, but falls again. "I'm too pumped," he says. "Dirt me."

"Let P.K. show you how it's done," Pinebox says, grinning at me as he lowers Slink.

I'm just getting my harness on and had not planned on warming up on a 5.12. Plus, I'd rather not jump into the competitive jousting and annoy anyone before I've extended my Eldorado invitation, and I won't do that until Daria gets here. So I just roll my eyes and concentrate on threading the buckle of my harness.

"P.K., give me a catch, then," says Pinebox.

"You're not going to take an hour on this one like you did last week, I hope," I say. I dearly love these guys, but they easily turn both me and Daria into belay slaves if given half a chance.

I stuff the rope into my belay device and clip myself into the anchor. That's when I spot him: long blond hair in a messy ponytail; broad shoulders with lanky, scarecrow arms and legs; and even from several yards away I can see he's got heart-stopping clear blue eyes. He is traveling sideways, bouldering around the perimeter of the wall just under the yellow "Do not boulder above this line" tape. He moves with such grace he makes me think of that sexy Russian ballet dancer. I know I have not seen him here before.

"Earth to P.K." Pinebox tugs on the rope. "Am I on belay?"

I snap out of my staring. "Belay is on," I say.

As Pinebox starts up the wall, I focus. Wouldn't want to drop him just before I ask him to run away with me. But the Russian-dancer guy is coming closer on his route around the wall, and I can't help sneaking peeks at him.

TWELVE

CRITTER

Pleasure in movement.
Pleasure in balance.
Pleasure in defying gravity.

Pleasure in the grit of fake rock under my fingertips.

Pleasure in . . . oh, wow. *Nice* chest. Thank God for sports bras. Nice everything, actually, including mad dreads for a white girl. . . . Oops, I'm staring. Try not to linger on the . . . oh man, thank God for tight, stretchy pants, too. Uh-oh—staring again. Better employ sunglasses before she notices.

THIRTEEN

P.K.: So, what's with the sunglasses?

Critter: Um . . .

P.K.: I haven't seen you here before—you from out of town or something?

Critter: Um . . .

P.K.: Do you speak English?

Pinebox: Up rope! P.K., are you paying attention?

P.K.: Sorry.

Pinebox: I'm going to go for it here. You got me?

P.K.: I've got you.

Critter: Yes.

P.K.: Huh?

Critter: I was answering your question.

P.K.: What question?

Pinebox: Falling!

P.K.: Shake it out and try again. You'll get it.

Pinebox: Would you quit talking down there so I know you've got me?

P.K.: All right, fine.

Critter: Later.

P.K.: Later.

FOURTEEN

P.K.

He's even hotter up close. And now he's off bouldering along the wall again. But what am I thinking? I'm *leaving*. Even if he did just move here, even if he does have killer blue eyes and a body to match, even if he is an awesome climber, it doesn't matter. I'm out of here.

FIFTEEN

CRITTER

Fifteen minutes and I'll have circled around the entire gym and back to where she is.

Must think of a better pickup line than "Um."

SIXTEEN

P.K.

Daria finally arrives, Pinebox comes down from the climb (cursing because he couldn't get the move), and I pop the Eldo question. I am met with seriously lame excuses.

Slink: I've got to find a summer job—my credit cards are through the roof.

Adam: My parents want me to start college applications—you know, the whole "prep for law school" thing.

And finally, Pinebox with the worst excuse of all: I don't know, P.K. Are you sure this is a good idea? I mean, if your parents catch up to us, they'll hate me forever.

I want to scream, but I don't. I start to take off my harness, making it clear I'm not going to hang out and climb with this sorry group of nonfriends. The guys kind of shuffle their feet and won't look at me. Daria comes over to hug me, and I let her, and it makes me feel like crying.

"P.K., I wish I could go with you—really," says Adam.

"Then why don't you?" I snap.

There is total, uncomfortable silence. Then I blurt out, "You guys are going to follow all the rules laid down on you and you're going to get into college and pay your bills and one day you're going to wake up and wonder why you never just *went* for it—why you never lived your own life instead of the life somebody else wanted you to live, why you couldn't just go on one absolutely incredible adventure when you were young and when someone you *said* was your friend needed you to go." I don't even know what I'm saying, don't even know if I believe the words that are coming out of my mouth, but I'm half crying and more than half angry, and then suddenly there he is, standing calmly, no sunglasses, blue eyes looking right at me.

"I'll go."

SEVENTEEN

CRITTER

Can I help it if they're the most amazing bunch of idiots I've ever seen? I mean, this drop-dead cute girl is actually begging for someone to run away with her, and they've all got better things to do. Not that she's a damsel in distress—she's got a stance like a bulldog when she's angry, which she is right now, and all I can do is wait to see if she either says "fine" or slugs me.

EIGHTEEN

Pinebox: Who the hell are you?

Adam: Bug off, man—this isn't a public hearing. Does she even *know* you?

Daria: Chill, guys. Do you think we know every

single person P.K. is friends with? P.K., introduce us?

Slink: You're an awesome climber, man. You want to hop on this five-twelve we're working?

P.K. (*dazedly*): I'm leaving tomorrow morning. . . . I know that's short notice. . . .

Critter: I'm on it. Meet you here? Early?

P.K.: *Nodding.*

Daria: Hello? What just happened here?

NINETEEN

P. K.

And he walks out the door, just like that, kind of like an apparition. I'm left to make up a whole lot of lies about how he's a friend of my cousin's and his name is Paul and I was really surprised to see him here because he told me he only climbs outdoors, but I'm sure he'll be a great guy to do this trip with because my cousin (do I even *have* a cousin?) has always said good things about him. Daria is eyeing me and I think she knows I'm lying. But she also completely trusts me, and my judgment, and I can almost hear her thinking that if I'm comfortable taking a trip with this guy—whoever he is—then she's good with it. So why *am* I fine with running off with this "Paul" person? Something in his eyes tells me he is not an ax murderer, not a rapist, and that he is a better-than-average Sherpa. He seems trustworthy, except for the fact that he walked out wearing rental rock shoes—

probably just an oversight. And he seems, well, *nice*.

Or maybe I just can't resist running away with a gorgeous blue-eyed stranger.

TWENTY

CRITTER

It's not exactly *stealing*, it's more of a long-term rental. I couldn't have left on a climbing trip with this girl without rock shoes. I'll return them when we get caught and are sent back here.

I consider the night's lodging options:

> A. Cardboard box hauled out of Dumpster behind climbing gym (could be cold).
> B. Lawn chair display in twenty-four-hour Walmart (lights awfully bright).
> C. A nice, long, all-night walk around the warehouse district (sounds tiring).
> D. Use part of Jenna's hundred dollars to pay for a motel room (what a waste).

But that's later. First, dining options:

> 1. Fast food (good grease level, sticks with you).
> 2. Actual restaurant (again, a waste).

3. The Dumpster again (could be risky).

4. Walk to a bar; order a glass of water; fill up on pretzels, peanuts, and maraschino cherries until I get kicked out for nonconsumption of alcohol (jackpot!).

TWENTY-ONE

P. K.

Can it be that you only really appreciate your parents when you're about to leave them? Dad insists on looking at the glossy brochure from the new school with me. He's really enthusiastic (maybe *he* wants to go there?). I tune out what he's saying, but I am aware of *him*, his presence. He's like a bridge you can trust, not shaky or swaying, just solid. He's always there, quiet and stubborn and reliable. I breathe in his smell: very faint aftershave from this morning, and that minty gum he always chews. It's all so familiar. His words are like blah-blah-blah-blah-blah, you could join the lacrosse team, the girls look really nice, don't you think some of these boys look handsome? Yada yada. But his presence is like something precious, a part of my home, and it tugs on my heart. It's not that he's a bad father, it's just that he doesn't get it, doesn't get *me*. And there's no way to make him get it.

When I'm lying on my bed, about to go to sleep, Mom comes in. (Actually, I'm about to pretend to go to sleep—I've got a lot of packing to do, and I'll take a middle-of-the-night bike ride to the climbing gym to drop stuff off, then back past the ATM to pick up cash.) Mom sits on my bed, smoothes my hair, and makes her usual comment that she wishes I'd let her comb out my dreadlocks so she can brush my hair like she used to. I tell her for the hundredth time that dreads don't comb out, you have to cut them off if you want to grow out normal hair again, but I'm not as annoyed by her as usual. I actually have a twinge that it would be nice to sit and have her brush my hair the way she did when I was younger.

"I'm sorry you'll be leaving us," she says.

I nearly have a heart attack, until I realize she means leaving for boarding school. "Me, too," I say, and I mean it.

"It was hard enough having the boys go off to college, but I thought you'd be with us for another few years, you know?" She gets choked up, and I give her a quick hug and a kiss on the cheek. "Good night, Mom," I say. "I better get some sleep." She sniffles as she leaves my room.

So that I don't have to think about sad parents anymore, I focus on the list of things that go into each backpack—mine and Tom's old one, the one he rejected because Mom sewed a University of Vermont logo on it and he ended up going to Penn State. My pack has got emblems from a bunch of different national parks on it: Grand Canyon, Yellowstone, Everglades. It's a little dorky, but my mom loves sewing things on our packs, so I figure let her do it if it makes her happy.

I never got to talk to the "Paul" guy about who was bringing what, so I pack pretty much everything just in case. My plan is to sneak out with my bike and take the packs—hang one on my back and one on my chest—to the gym and stash them near the Dumpster. Then the "Paul" guy and I can get them in the morning after I tell my parents I'm going out for a run. We can sort out what gear we need and what we've got doubles of, and leave Tom's pack with the extra gear at the gym for Daria to pick up.

TWENTY-TWO

". . . there is nothing either good or bad, but thinking makes it so."

Hamlet by William Shakespeare

TWENTY-THREE

CRITTER

Dawn.

Always a good reminder of the perfection of all things. It's like the earth waking up again to say, "I'm here—what's not to like?"

Of course, if you let it, your mind will come in a second later with a whole list of things not to like. But I stopped letting my mind do that awhile ago.

Chilly. I rub my hands together, going for the friction

heat source. Steam rises in a cloud as I take a piss. The sky is a beautiful orange-red: city air pollution–induced sunrise art.

There's still enough water in my to-go cup for a drink, face washing, and teethbrushing.

I wonder if she'll actually show up?

TWENTY-FOUR

P. K.

Oh God, he's got that sexy tousled look like he's slept in his clothes or something.

"Hey," I say.

"Hey," he says.

I wasn't sure he'd be here, and I can tell from his surprised look that he wasn't at all sure I'd show up either.

"Where's your stuff?" I ask.

"In my pockets," he says, helpfully pulling out a T-shirt, toothbrush, deodorant, and some crumpled-up cash.

"Very funny," I say. "I mean your gear. We need to figure out what we've got doubles of, since I brought tons of stuff— tent, camp stove, rope, cams. . . ." My list slows down as the blank look on his face tells me I have just seen all of his gear. I push away thoughts of what might make someone show up for an extended climbing trip with only a toothbrush. I take some comfort in the fact that I don't think convicts remember the "change of T-shirt and deodorant" thing when they break out of prison. At least we won't be lugging anything extra around.

"I brought most of what we need anyway," I say. I show him the two packs hidden behind the Dumpster. "I came here in the middle of the night to stash these. It was kind of creepy—there was this homeless person curled up in that cardboard box over there. I just dropped the packs and got out of here as quick as I could."

He nods.

I hope he's not, like, terminally shy. He grabs the bigger of the two packs, clips his climbing shoes onto the outside, and hoists it onto his back. I throw my pack on as well. There's the din of city traffic in the background. Any one of those cars can take us out of town, west, away from all the dos and don'ts my parents have for me, away from what I've always known. I am suddenly flooded with fear—what am I *doing*?

The "Paul" guy grins at me. "Are you ready?" he asks. "Just remember, there's nothing to be afraid of, anytime, ever. Life is one hundred percent adventure."

And for a moment I believe him, and we hike off toward the highway, ready to stick our thumbs out and see how far away from this place we can get.

TWENTY-FIVE

Conversation on way to major road out of town, toward Interstate 70:

So, my name's P.K.

I know. I heard your friends talking to you.

Pause

And your name is . . . ?

Critter.

Nice to meet you.

Yep.

Conversation upon arriving at major road:

Critter: We're only a few miles from your house, right? I mean you walked here this morning?

P.K.: I ran, yeah.

Critter: So, we start on the bus (pointing to bus stop sign) before any of your neighbors see us. That is, unless you want to get caught right away?

P.K.: *Why* would I want to get caught right away?!

Critter: I'm just *asking.*

Conversation on bus:

Conversation upon disembarking from city bus as close to Interstate 70 as possible:

Critter: Okay, now we hitchhike. But you stand over there like you're not with me in case it's your mom's tennis partner who pulls over.

P.K.: My mom doesn't play tennis.

Critter: Just give me the thumbs-up if the driver is safe, okay?

P.K.: Fine.

Conversation as driver of behemoth gray pickup truck pulls over:

Driver: You can throw that pack in the back, kid. How far you going?

Critter: To Interstate 70 and then west, sir.

Driver: You're in luck.

(*P.K. gives thumbs-up, Critter motions* come on.)

Driver: So there's *two* of you, huh? Well, pile on in, I got room.

Conversation upon disembarking from the third eighteen-wheeler of the day, at a truck stop many miles west, as night is falling:

Critter: You going to stay mad at me for the do-you-want-to-get-caught-right-away question for the whole trip?

P.K.: You don't even know me. What makes you think I'd want to get caught right away? It was a stupid, obnoxious thing to say.

Critter: No, it was logical.

P.K.: *What?*

Critter: You told all your friends, including that Daria girl, exactly where you're going. How long do you think it will take your parents to get the information out of them and come get you? My guess is Daria will hold out for two days, max. I just thought you might want to save them the trouble, and save yourself all these miles of hitching, that's all.

Conversation at greasy diner in truck stop:

P.K.: So, if I don't want to get caught, we can't go to Eldorado Canyon.

Critter: Right.

P.K.: Any other ideas?

Conversation with amphetamine-pumped driver of eighteen-wheeler who is about to leave truck stop:

A.P. driver: Where you headed?

Critter: Las Vegas. Actually, Red Rocks, but Vegas is close enough.

A.P. driver: Come on, I can get you most of the way there, and I'll be glad to have the company during the night.

TWENTY-SIX

CRITTER

We climb up into the cab with our packs, me first on the assumption that the driver will be less likely to want to grab my leg than hers. The drivers we've met so far have all been good guys, though. They talk about families and girlfriends, and how much they miss them. They chat on the CB with their bosses and other truckers in that alien-disc-jockey CB language. They chew tobacco and spit into Mountain Dew bottles.

This guy is definitely hyped. Says he's been driving solid since yesterday morning because he's trying to finish his run and make it home for his kid's birthday party. I figure we are either, A) being good Samaritans for helping him stay awake, or B) making an incredibly stupid decision to drive with anyone so sleep-deprived. I decide if he starts to fall asleep I'll grab *his* leg.

P.K. is tired—I can feel her energy start to lag. (Am I hooked into her energy already?) "You can sleep," I tell her. "I'll sit up." She nods, puts her head back, and closes her eyes.

"So, how old is your kid?" I ask Jimmy, our chauffeur.

"Five. He turned five last week, but the party is tomorrow so I can be there. He's the smartest kid in his kindergarten class, you know that? He knows his letters already. . . ."

And he is off on a manic account of all of his kid's accomplishments, including finally conquering bed-wetting. I figure as long as he's talking we're good, so I turn my attention back to P.K., just to notice her. When we pass another truck, the light moves across her face. She's even cuter asleep. All that fight is forgotten and she's gentler. She's got a peach-colored glow around her—must be her signature color. Her head starts to tip toward my shoulder and I will it to keep moving . . . *yes*. Very nice. Her hair smells like some kind of herbal shampoo. I stare out the windshield at the oncoming traffic and the taillights up ahead. Why do I feel like it's my job to protect her? Probably some sort of genetically imprinted data from the Neolithic age. It feels good, though. Not all instinctive impulses need to be wrestled into political correctness. She shifts, gets more comfortable on my shoulder. I wonder if she's totally asleep, or if she's at least partly aware of what she's doing, snuggling in like that. I smile. This *is* going to be an adventure.

TWENTY-SEVEN

P. K.

"No no no no no!"

The trucker's outburst drags me out of sleep. I straighten up and shove Critter's head off my lap. All right, so I remember doing a little innocent snuggling into his shoulder last night, but who gave him permission to lie all over me?

"Get out of here! You both got to get out!"

The truck's not moving and the truck driver is frantically pushing at Critter, who is groggily yawning like he has not just been shoved first from one direction and then the other.

"Okay, man," Critter says. "Hey, thanks for the ride. Have fun at your kid's birthday party."

I fumble for the door handle.

The trucker groans. "That's the *problem*. I'll never make it now. I pulled over here to take a quick nap, and I must have slept for hours. Look at that, it's getting light. Aw geez. I'll miss the whole party. My wife is going to kill me. Go on, get out. I got to drive like a maniac now—can't have you kids needing a pee break or a drop-off."

I get the door open and we tumble out, packs and all.

The truck peels out, as much as an eighteen-wheeler can peel, and leaves us in a cloud of dawn-lit roadside dust. I look around at where we are: two-lane back road, not a single vehicle in sight, rolling open fields of scrub vegetation in every direction, no houses.

Critter stretches, reaching his arms to the sky, smiling. "Look how perfect it is," he says, his voice tinged with the kind of wonder normally reserved for miracles.

I look around one more time, just to make sure I'm not missing something. Then I let him have it. "What are you talking about? We're in the middle of nowhere, we don't even know where nowhere *is*, there are no cars coming by to get us out of here, and you think it's perfect? Are you *insane*?"

"Apparently," he says.

"Don't get all sarcastic with me. Just figure out a way to get us out of here." I know I'm sounding royally obnoxious, and suddenly I don't even know why I'm being that way, except that I'm angry about finding his head in my lap when I woke up. But to be fair, I was also slumped over him, so maybe it all just happened in our sleep.

He turns away from me to take a piss, and so I go find a place to squat to do the same. When I come back, I feel better. "Okay, so we need to find a way out of Oz, right?" I say it nicely, the closest I can get to an apology.

"Actually," he says, "I think we might be in Kansas."

I give him half a smile, and he grins. That's when I see it: speck of sun like an orange star on the horizon; wispy clouds of pink and lavender; insects switching posts, some going to sleep, some just waking up, making the air alive; breeze moving the scrub grass so it looks like it's dancing . . . and I am filled with wonder. I take a deep breath and turn slowly, letting each bit of it greet my senses. When I turn to face Critter, he sees it in my eyes.

"I told you," he says softly.

TWENTY-EIGHT

CRITTER

She sees it.

She *saw* it, anyway, at least for a moment, before she started thinking and problem solving and figuring out a way to get us back to civilization and on to our "destination." For a second, she knew it: that there is no future destination, only *here*, and there is actually no future or past at all, only *now*. And *now* is perfect.

But meanwhile, back to the adventure: we figure out that the din in the distance is, in fact, not a waterfall (since there seems to be no water and nothing for it to fall off of in these parts) but a major highway. We deduce logically that Jimmy would not have driven too far off the highway (which we hope is either Interstate 70 or 40—we'll be happy with either one) to take a nap. So we figure we can walk toward the noise, which is also the direction Jimmy went, and eventually end up somewhere from which we can get to Las Vegas. We eat some crackers, which we saved from our soup dinner last night, drink some water, pick up Toto (just kidding), and start hiking.

TWENTY-NINE

Conversation on hike toward waterfall-like sound:

P.K.: We've had very cool drivers, all of them of the nonrapist, nonmurderer variety. What are the chances of *that*?

Critter: One hundred percent. Since it already *is*, it follows the Law of Inevitability.

P.K.: You mean like everything is plotted out and we can't change anything? Like predestination?

Critter: No way. We can change whatever we want, just not anything that has already happened.

P.K.: Well, duh.

THIRTY

Conversation near mining-type operation that, from a distance, was making an unmistakable waterfall/heavy traffic noise:

P.K.: We're screwed.

Critter: Not hardly.

THIRTY-ONE

CRITTER

That's when I blow it. I mean, just totally blow it big-time.

Me: All we have to do is figure out what we want, track it, and pull it in.

Her: Huh?

Me: We're on a road, aren't we? We want a ride, right? So, imagine it and bring it on.

Her: *Huh?*

Me (on extremely false assumption that, just because she had one moment of clarity at sunrise, she's ready for the full Expanded Reality lecture): Look, stuff isn't solid *or* predetermined. It's all just (waving my hands as visual aids) protons and electrons in orbit, mostly empty space—it's infinite possibility waiting for us to decide what we want, track it, and pull it in. You want a truck, we can have a truck. I was thinking more along the lines of maybe a family driving kids to dance class or soccer or whatever, you know, totally safe and homey. I'd like to get you to Red Rocks without having to slug anybody.

She just stands there with her mouth gaping open. That's when I have a chance, one slender chance, to backpedal real quick, tell her I was just messing with her, but it couldn't hurt to think positive, something like that. But instead, I dig the hole deeper. I show her the cloud trick.

"Look, I'll show you how it works. Pick a cloud, maybe a small one to start with," I tell her.

She hasn't closed her mouth yet, but she looks up and points to a wispy streak. Piece of cake.

"All right," I say. "Send it heat. I'll help you, and we'll make it disappear."

"Send it heat?" she asks slowly. I can't tell if she's just dumbfounded, or starting to get scared of me.

"Really. Watch, I'll do it." I look at the cloud, send my energy out as heat to dry it up, and it disappears in seconds.

P.K. backs away from me, frowning. Then she tips her head and crosses her arms over her chest. "You know something about clouds, right? That they disappear in the morning? Or that the little ones are always disappearing?"

Thank God I come to my senses then. Instead of demonstrating for her how I can pick which cloud to make disappear, or showing her that she can do it, too, I bring her back to our basic problem, which is *not* the fact that there are a few wispy clouds in the sky. "Let's keep on walking," I say. "We'll get to the highway eventually."

We walk and she is quiet. Her walls are up. I've totally freaked her. Well, it's done. The Law of Inevitability in action.

In the meantime, I picture it: dark-blue minivan, a bunch of kids, nice mom or dad, plenty of room for two teenagers and two large backpacks.

THIRTY-TWO

P.K.

First I find his head in my lap, and now he's gone delusional. And we're lost in the middle of nowhere. I guess we could have tried to find a human at the place with all the industrial equipment, but now we're walking away from there, too. I get a sudden twinge of homesickness. Wish I could call Daria. But I left my cell phone in my room on my desk—couldn't deal with the guilt of having it and *not* using it to call anyone. If I'd brought it with me, I'm sure I would have gotten a dozen voice messages already: "Hey, P.K., this is Adam. Sorry I couldn't go with you. Is that guy really a friend of your cousin's? Daria says she didn't know you had any cousins." *Click.* Daria's voice: "P.K. Call me. Your parents and my parents are driving me *crazy* with questions about where you went." *Click.* "Hi, honey, it's Mom. Just checking in to see how your escape is going. Call me when you get a chance between rides with truckers, okay? Dad sends his love. Bye." *Click.*

I sigh. This is not turning out to be the romantic, exciting, all-you-can-climb adventure I had hoped for. I glance at Critter. He seems deep in thought. Maybe he's creating clouds, because a bunch of gray ones are amassing up ahead. That's all we need to make the nightmare complete: rain.

I stop and put down my pack so I can fish out my rain gear. Critter starts walking backward, smiling and waving. At first I think he has totally gone off the deep end, but then I look behind us: vehicle!

Oh my God, finally a car. We *can't* let this one pass us. I join Critter in waving, making large "We're hitchhiking, see?" motions with our thumbs, jumping up and down. It's a light-blue minivan with a bunch of kids peering out the windows. It comes closer and slows to a stop. I have never been so happy to see a Dodge Grand Caravan.

THIRTY-THREE

CRITTER

Okay, so I was slightly off on the color.

The driver—must be the dad—leans over the mom and yells out the passenger window, "What the heck are you doing out *here*?"

I can't think of an answer, but P.K. smiles at the kids and says, "We got dropped here by a tornado."

Nobody seems to get the *Wizard of Oz* reference—at least nobody laughs. The kids just stare at us with wide eyes. There's five of them, all different ages.

"Go on, don't just gawk, open the door and let them in," the dad says.

An older girl, maybe twelve or thirteen, slides open the van door.

"You kids pile in back, let these two up front. I want to talk to them," says the dad.

The kids obediently climb to the backseats, the two littlest on laps, and leave the seats just behind the driver for us. They're all dressed in an old-fashioned way, the girls in long flowered dresses, the boys in black slacks and white shirts. We stuff our packs under our feet and pull the door shut. The dad turns to get a good look at us. He looks right at P.K. and gives a low whistle. "Is this what happened to hairstyles in the past year?" he asks. At first I think he's being facetious, but then I see he's just asking.

One of the little girls touches P.K.'s dreads, then snatches her hand back. P.K. grins at her. "You can touch them," she says, but the little girl doesn't reach out again.

"Where's my manners?" the dad says. "I'm Leroy; this here is my wife Ruth." The tired-looking fortyish woman in the front seat smiles, and I see she is missing a tooth. "And those are some of my kids back there."

"They're all yours?" P.K. asks, amazed.

"You've got *others*?" I ask, equally amazed.

"Yep." Leroy nods. "Got twenty-four all told. But the rest are growed."

The van rumbles into motion as Leroy starts driving. He also starts talking, and we find out why he wanted us up close. The man can *talk*, and from the sound of it, he doesn't get out much and he's thrilled to have a new audience to listen to him.

"What on earth brought you out on that road?" he asks, but he doesn't give time for an answer, just plunges ahead. "Hardly anybody uses that road—it leads to our town, which is pretty much all fundamentalists, and they don't go out of town, and nobody from the outside comes in except a delivery truck from time to time. But I'm what they call an apostate, which means I got excommunicated from the church awhile back. Not for doing anything bad, mind you, but for having some original ideas. Like when the church leaders were preaching hellfire and brimstone years back, at the turn of the millennium, and they said that God was going to smite all of the godless masses, I took a bunch of my kids—a different passel of them then, since some of those are grown now; Sarah, you were there, but you was just a baby. Anyway, I took them off to Las Vegas for New Year's Eve. We watched the ball drop along with the godless masses, and God didn't smite anybody. I wanted my kids to see that, so they'd know that the church isn't always right. Since then we go back to Las Vegas once a year, you know why?"

"So the kids can see that the godless masses are still alive?" I ask.

"No," says Leroy. "Cheap food. I can feed this whole vanfull. . . . Kids, how many of you are back there?" he calls.

There is a moment of counting, and the kids start to call out, "Five!" "Five." "Five." And the littlest boy calls out, "Four!"

"Ronnie, you have to count yourself, too," one of his sisters tells him.

"Anyway, I can feed this whole bunch for next to nothing—all you can eat, at the Palm Gardens. The little ones are free."

I see P.K. eyeing Ruth, and when Leroy takes a breather, P.K. shoots a question at her. "You had twenty-four babies?"

Ruth shakes her head real quick, and Leroy starts talking again.

"Nope, they're not all her kids; they're all mine, though. I used to have three wives, you know, following the church's teachings and all. But when I went apostate, two of my wives walked out. They left the kids with me. But Ruthie here stayed." He puts his hand on Ruth's knee, and she pats it and smiles.

P.K.'s eyes are wide. "You had three wives?" she blurts out. In the short time I've known her, I've never known P.K. to be diplomatic. "That's *totally* weird. And Ruth had to raise those other women's children?"

I elbow her and try to give her a mental message: *Don't insult the driver or we'll be out on the street, and it will be a* year *before anyone drives by again.*

But Leroy is unfazed. "I know, I know. I seen on TV that the rest of the world thinks it's weird, but if it's the way you're raised . . ."

One of the boys interrupts from the backseat. "Daddy's going to get us a TV," he says.

"Yeah," the other kids chime in.

"We're getting a TV," little Ronnie says. "We're getting a postate TV."

P.K. laughs. "A prostate TV?"

Leroy clarifies. "He's saying 'an apostate TV.' Only apostates have them, because having a TV is against the church's teaching."

"Well, when you get it you should watch *The Wizard of Oz*," P.K. says.

"What's that?" Leroy asks.

"It's a movie. It's from an amazing book by L. Frank Baum, and they show it every year," she says.

"Aaron, write that down," Leroy shouts back. "*The Wizard of Is.*"

"Oz," P.K. corrects.

Aaron, who must be about ten, sticks his tongue out in concentration as he writes in big scrawly letters in a note-book.

"The older ones have got to write about what they see in Las Vegas," Leroy says. "So they don't forget."

It dawns on me that my tracking and pulling-in might have worked even better than I thought. "Are you going to Vegas *now*?" I ask.

"Yes siree," says Leroy. "Our annual trip. We do it in May now instead of New Year's. Food's even cheaper when the weather turns hot. We'll be there in four or five hours, just in time for lunch."

So it turns out we were a lot farther west than Kansas. I cross my arms over my chest and sit back. Sweeeet.

THIRTY-FOUR

Conversation after being dropped off by Leroy in midtown Las Vegas:

Critter: We could have taken him up on his lunch offer and *then* ditched them. I mean come on, free food? Where's your survival instinct?

P.K.: It's just too creepy. Those poor kids. Can you imagine living with three mothers in one house?

Critter: Yeah. Every night before dinner it would be: "Wash your hands." "Wash your hands." "Wash your hands." And before bed: "Brush your teeth." "Brush your teeth." "Brush your teeth."

P.K.: It's not funny!

Critter: Come on, chill. It's not those kids who had to live with it anyway. The oldest ones in that van were only babies when the two wives left him. Come to think of it, it's a great insurance policy. I mean, the guy had *two* wives leave him and he's still got one. *Ow!*

THIRTY-FIVE

P. K .

I shake out my hand then stretch my fingers.

"All right, no more polygamist jokes," Critter says, rubbing his arm where I slugged him.

"Thank you," I say.

And then I'm embarrassed at having stooped to violence to get my way. "Sorry," I begin, "I'm just . . ." I start to take a physical assessment, and the list quickly becomes very long: I'm hungry, thirsty, weary, hot and sweaty, a little scared, and I stink. I sigh. "Do you think we could find a restroom, wash up, and then go get lunch?"

"Absolutely," he says.

He's not even copping an attitude about me punching him, and that's a relief.

The streets are swarming with people in colorful T-shirts and shorts. The sun beats down, dry and hot, and my pack feels like it has gained a few pounds. There are signs everywhere advertising live shows, casinos, restaurants. Huge digital screens flash with everything from dancing bodies to wild horses. Critter starts up some steps, and I look at the sign above his head.

"That's a casino," I say.

"Everything in town is a casino," he says. "And people in casinos need bathrooms and food."

I trudge up the steps after him. Inside we are greeted with frosty air-conditioning, the din of distant slot machines, and a guy handing out flyers for a live band performance.

Our eyes slowly adjust to the windowless but festive lighting. We wander past the entrance to a section with video poker machines, roulette wheels, cocktail waitresses wearing little outfits that involve sheer black stockings and thongs, and a guy checking IDs so no one underage can get past him. Critter stares at one of the waitresses. Actually, he stares at her butt.

"That's my goal in life," I say. "To get a job where I don't have to walk around with my heinie hanging out."

Critter laughs, then he points happily. We've found the restrooms.

In the ladies' room I haul off my shirt and soap up my armpits. I do it fast before I get caught acting like a street person. Just as I'm drying off with a wad of paper towels, the door swings open and a woman walks in. Busted. I grab my clean shirt, pull it on real quick, and go to hoist my pack.

"Hey, the climbing gym has showers, you know," the woman says.

I freeze in midhoist. "The climbing gym?" I parrot her.

"Yeah. That's where I work. I'm heading out there to start my shift in about an hour. You got a car?"

I shake my head.

She goes into a stall and keeps talking to me as she pees. "I can give you a ride. My boyfriend and I were hanging out here on the strip this morning, but now he's gone to work and I'm getting lunch." She flushes and comes out of the stall. "They've got a great buffet here." She looks at me in the mirror as she washes her hands. "I bet you'll find someone either at the gym or at the climbing shop next door who's headed out to the rocks and the campground. That is where you're going, right?"

I nod, amazed at this woman's perception and at our good luck. I stick out my hand. "Hi, I'm P.K. I really appreciate your help."

"I'm Melanie," she says, shaking my hand. "Glad to do it."

THIRTY-SIX

Critter, while washing up, in between dancing a disco/breakdance hybrid number and singing snatches of the song being piped into the men's room:

That's the way, uh-huh, uh-huh, I like it. Track it, yeah! Pull it in, woo! Sock it to me, sock it to me, sock it to me. I want a *big* lunch, uh-huh, uh-huh, I like it. . . . I want a ride to the rocks, uh-huh, uh-huh, I like it. Yeah! Oh, and a place to sleep that's better than a box, better than a truck, uh-huh, uh-huh—

(Performance is aborted by bouncer-sized neckless wonder entering the men's room.)

THIRTY-SEVEN

P.K.

We follow Melanie to what has to be the biggest and least expensive all-you-can-eat buffet on the planet. I'm talking southern food, Chinese food, Mexican, pizza, ribs, pasta, salad bar, and on and on. While Critter eats more than any human I've ever seen, Melanie wants to hear all about our climbing histories.

I tell her how I first climbed at the gym on Daria's twelfth birthday when she had her party there, and the addiction started that day. Yeah, I'm a gym rat, I admit, but I also get outdoors whenever we can find someone with a car who will take us. And I make it clear that I've taken both the basic and the intermediate trad lead courses, and that I've led lots of 5.10s and even a few 11s. I don't want Melanie to start cautioning us about doing the trad climbs in Red Rocks or giving any other motherly type warnings. Not that she's so old—she must be early thirties, petite, with short dark hair.

It's just that I don't want to hear a *should* or *shouldn't* from anyone right now.

"So, are you guys on summer break?" Melanie asks. "Do you go to school around here?"

I'm assuming she means college, since I don't know of any high schools that get out in May, so I commence lying. "Yeah, summer break. Actually we go to school back east." I don't know what colleges are around Vegas, so I figure "back east" is safe.

"Really? Where?" she asks innocently.

I endure a moment of silent inner panic. "University of . . ."

Critter sees my moment, and comes to the rescue. "Nobleboro," he says with his mouth full of fried chicken.

"University of Nobleboro?" she says. "Never heard of it."

"It's a small school," Critter says.

"Very small," I say.

Melanie nods and picks up a short rib. She doesn't ask where the school is located, but I feel confident that Critter would have an answer for that.

"So, tell me about yourself, Critter," she says. "How did you get into climbing?"

It occurs to me that I still know almost nothing about him. I listen intently as he tells of having first climbed at the gym in Springfield—the one I go to—with his dad when he was about nine. But then his family moved to upstate New York, to a small town with no climbing gym. He didn't find out until a few years later that he was actually living near a primo trad climbing area, namely the Shawangunks. He got hooked up with some older guys who had cars and for a couple of years went to the Gunks every weekend.

"But a year ago we moved back again to Springfield, and . . ."

It's like a dark cloud crosses his face. His eyes shift. Then he shrugs.

"And I haven't climbed much since then," he says. He takes a huge bite of mashed potatoes, so that just in case anybody wants to ask any clarifying questions, they're going to have to look at mashed potatoes and spit in order to hear an answer. Needless to say, neither Melanie nor I ask him anything.

"Well, you two sound like you're experienced enough and skilled enough to conquer Red Rocks," Melanie says.

So she *was* being a mother hen.

"I've got a question for you," I say. "How did you know I was a climber right off the bat?"

Melanie laughs. "Tourists and high rollers don't usually wash up in the restrooms, and the prostitutes don't normally carry huge backpacks with carabiners clipped on the outside."

THIRTY-EIGHT

CRITTER

No way P.K. can handle the whole story. She got weirded out enough about clouds, Expanded Reality, and a little polygamy. She doesn't like things that are too far off the beaten track. If I told her what I did and where I went and how it landed me in the psych ward, she'd totally freak. I'm *not* telling her. Case closed. On to my burrito.

THIRTY-NINE

P.K.

Melanie is really helpful, though I'm not sure if I like her anymore since I think she pretty much almost called me a whore. Anyway, she says she has to pick up a few things at the grocery store on her way to work, so Critter and I run around the store and grab what we need: pasta, instant oatmeal, soup, propane, peanut butter, apples, underwear and socks for Critter because I tell him I won't climb with him if he doesn't have a change of undies. Then at the climbing gym, just like Melanie said, we meet this guy Dante, who is also there for a shower and to wash his dirty clothes in the sink, and then he's driving back out to the campground. We ask if we can hitch a ride and he says, "Sure."

Dante is short and stocky, with muscular arms and chest. He's the kind of climber who will complain about being "height challenged" and then have so much power he can pull off the moves anyway. He and Critter are already doing the "where I've climbed and how hard I climb" guy thing. Dante has definitely got some major ego going on. But he's got wheels, which is the most important thing to us right now.

With clean, wet clothes hanging on the outside of our packs, and our hair smelling of shampoo, we pile into Dante's beat-up Land Rover and follow the two-lane highway out of Las Vegas, into the high desert landscape of dusty brown mountains and pale-green scrub bushes. Critter talks about how he and I are looking for some good long 5.10 or 5.11 trad routes to get on, and Dante says he'll hook us up. As the afternoon sun moves across the sky, Dante takes us on the loop road so we can see the rocks. They rise up off the desert floor, formations eight hundred, a thousand, even two thousand feet high. They are jumbled, folded in on themselves, with shadowed corners and brightly lit arêtes. The sun catches the sandstone just right, making it glow deep red as if proving to anyone who might be watching that it deserves its name.

We get out of the car at a pull-off. Critter and Dante are busy talking about some new route Dante wants to put up deep in one of the canyons, but I am mesmerized by the rocks. I am drawn to them. I want to be out there in that world where rock and sky and wind become all-that-is, and my brain gives up its endless circles. I know the rocks can clear my mind of worrying about how Mom and Dad are reacting, wondering if Daria is scared, trying to figure out if the police can possibly track me down if my parents file a missing-person report. . . . The rocks will take all of that and transform it into peace.

"Can we go out today?" I ask, interrupting the guys' conversation.

Dante shakes his head. "Can't. It rained yesterday, so you

can't climb today or the holds break off. The rain sinks into the sandstone and makes it soft. It's park rules."

I nod and look out at the rocks again. *I'll be back tomorrow*, I promise myself.

FORTY

CRITTER

The rocks are powerful. I feel them pulling me into their three-hundred-million-years-ago-I-used-to-be-an-ocean-floor presence. I nearly disappear into them, but Dante's chatter yanks me back. New routes to be had. Untouched rock deep in the canyon. Too cold in the winter; now the weather is perfect. His girlfriend is coming to put up a new route with him. All I can think is, *Spend the day climbing those amazing rocks, spend the night with a hot girl, what could be better?*

FORTY-ONE

P.K.

We drive back to the campground with the sun sinking low. There are no trees, just lots of sand and some desert shrubs, a primitive outhouse, and an outdoor water spigot. We find a campsite near where Dante is camped.

"You guys need any stuff?" Dante asks as we pile out of the car. "I've got tons of extra gear. Here." He throws a jacket at Critter. "You'll need this when the sun goes down."

"You got a harness?" Critter asks.

"Harness, belay device, chalk bag, CamelBak, whatever you need," says Dante. He rummages through duffel bags in his trunk.

"Sleeping bag?" Critter asks.

"You've got one," I say. "It's in your pack. I brought it just in case. Sleeping pad, too." It's my brother Tom's old gear, the stuff my mom almost sent to the Salvation Army. The "just in case" was in case Critter conveniently forgot his sleeping gear and then was like, "Oh, baby, I guess I'll have to share with you." That was before I knew him at all.

We unload our groceries and I hear Critter mumbling, "Oatmeal, soap, underwear, *dang*—helmet."

"Got one," says Dante. "I had a couple new guys here climbing with me last week, so I brought lots of extra stuff."

And just like that, the boy who left on an extended camping and climbing trip with little more than a toothbrush is totally outfitted.

I set up the tent while Critter builds a fire in the fire pit. Even the firewood has been mysteriously left there by the previous occupants.

"Everything you need just seems to come to you," I say.

"Yep," he says matter-of-factly. "Hey, you want me to start up the stove? We can heat that soup for dinner."

"Sounds perfect," I say.

Dante leaves us to go make some phone calls. The moon

rises in a clear, starry sky; the fire crackles. We eat our soup and stare into the flames, quiet and comfortable together. It's strange to think I've only known Critter for a couple days. It feels more like we've been friends for a long time.

In the silence, my worries start to creep in: Mom, Dad, Daria. Do my brothers know I'm gone yet? What are they all thinking? And with the worries comes the longing for the rocks, for peace.

"When you climb, does it . . ." I search for the words to express what I mean. "Take your mind and quiet it down?"

Critter's face is only partly lit by the firelight, but I see him perk up. "Yes," he says. "It's like it makes me disappear."

"Yes!" I say. It's so amazing to have someone understand.

"It lets the hamster out of the cage," he adds.

Now I'm not so sure we're on the same wavelength after all. "The *hamster*?" I ask.

"Yeah, it's like your mind is a hamster running on a wheel. Same old thoughts, day in and day out. You don't really get anywhere except maybe an occasional breakthrough. When I climb, all there's room for is the concentration on the gear and the next move. The thoughts stop, the wheel stops . . . the hamster is free."

I *get* it. I nod. Then, suddenly, I'm confused. "But, am *I* the hamster? Or is my mind the hamster, or the wheel, or what?"

Critter laughs. "Don't think about it too hard or you'll be back on the wheel."

FORTY-TWO

CRITTER

She *does* get it. Parts of it, anyway. I watch her, huddled up to the fire, the light dancing on her face. She's so . . . vulnerable.

I glance at the tent and I can't help it—I see me lying down next to her, stroking the side of her face with my fingertips, her taking a shuddery breath, me kissing her deeply. . . .

I stop my imagination right there, before she sees it in my eyes.

P.K. yawns. "I'm beat," she says.

"Me, too," I say quickly. I start to clean off the picnic table like a revved-up busboy, making it clear that's where I'm sleeping.

"You setting up out here?" she asks. "I don't mind sharing the tent. I do it with Pinebox and Adam and those guys all the time."

"I'm fine," I say. "I like sleeping under the stars." Which is true. Also true is the fact that my protective instincts are still operative, and tonight I am protecting her from *me*.

FORTY-THREE

P.K.

What just happened? I could swear he was thinking about kissing me. And it would have been nice, too.

FORTY-FOUR

CRITTER

Things we are pretending don't exist:

1. A whole bunch of people looking for P.K.
2. A whole bunch of people, including *the* cops,* looking for me.
3. A finite amount of cash between us.
4. Therefore, a finite amount of time we'll be out here in the desert with no interference.
5. The fact that I seriously want to jump her bones.

the cops: the police who are after me as if I am a criminal, not just a runaway teenager

Things we are pretending *do* exist, which actually don't:

1. Time
2. Matter
3. The future
4. The past
5. Problems
6. Fear

FORTY-FIVE

P.K.

Some days you wake up and you think you know what to expect, and you're right. Other days, you're wrong. Like today, I thought Critter and I were going to climb a couple of classic routes like Unfinished Symphony and then Breakaway on the Refrigerator Wall.

"Stupid bimbo!" It's Dante's voice, and my sleepy mind shuffles through any and all reasons he could be talking about me. I decide he can't be, and snuggle deeper into my sleeping bag. Then I hear Critter shushing him, and their voices moving away from the tent. I doze off again.

The next thing I know, Critter is outside the tent. "P.K., you awake? We've got something to decide."

It's the first time in three days I actually have an opportunity for some decent sleep, and instead I've got to make decisions. I unzip the tent. "This better be worth waking up for," I say.

"Do we want to put up a new route with Dante?"

Put up a new route? That's the stuff of climbing lore; the people whose names are now in the climbing books, exploring uncharted territory, making history, touching rock that has never been touched by humans. . . . I realize this is not a decision one can make before visiting the outhouse and water spigot.

When I come back, Critter explains it to me. Dante's girlfriend (aka "stupid bimbo") was supposed to come out to climb with him this week. Instead, she broke up with him over the phone (after having slept with his best friend). He said to her, "But we're still doing the route, right?" because he's gotten this overnight permit to go into the canyon, and he's really hot to do the route. But she said no, she's not coming. He's totally pissed.

"Why would he want to climb with her after she's broken up with him *and* slept with his best friend?" I ask.

"Apparently the permits are not easy to get," Critter says.

It's all becoming clear to me. "So this is where we come in?"

"Yep," Critter says. "You want to do it? It's a *long* hike in, that's why the overnight permit. We've got three days to complete the route and get back out."

Part of me is saying, *Oh my God, a first ascent. What an incredible adventure. Not to mention the fact that I'd get my name in the guidebook and even get to help name the route and rate it. I'll lead several pitches and get to touch rock that's never been touched by another human. . . .* The rest of me is shouting objections: *Climbing off into space not knowing how hard it is up ahead? Not knowing how you'll get down? Not knowing either of your climbing partners for more than a couple of days? What if we get stuck? What if one of us gets hurt and we're way deep in the canyon? It's insanity!*

Critter is looking at me hard. I can see he wants to do it. Him and his "Life is all adventure" stuff. He says, "Don't think too hard about it. Just ask yourself this: what would you do if you weren't afraid?"

In an instant I know my answer. "That's easy," I say. "I'd go."

"Great!" Critter jumps up and heads toward Dante's campsite.

"But Critter," I call after him, "I *am* afraid!"

FORTY-SIX

CRITTER

Dante already has gear spread out everywhere—I see he is assuming we'll say yes—and he's prancing around it with this can't-forget-anything-or-we're-screwed look on his face. It's the first time I've noticed colors this bright around anyone in a while. He's got a rainbow of shooting color bursts coming out from his head and shoulders.

"You're excited about this, huh?" I say.

"Oh, *yeah*," he says. He runs one hand over his hair. It's the kind of close-cropped dark frizz that used to get kids called "Brillo head" in middle school. "We need doubles on cams, leaver biners in case we bail. I've got chlorine tabs and a water filter—just bring water for one day. There's streams in there. Ascenders! We need ascenders."

P.K. comes up to us quietly and stands there with her arms folded. Dante's rainbow bursts must have turned on my color monitor, because I can see the boiling gray-black of fear swirling around her. I stand in front of her and put one hand on each of her shoulders, trying to press calmness back into her. Her colors momentarily turn toward her normal pastel peach, but then the gray-black creeps back in. How can I explain it to her? "P.K.," I say, "you're standing in a campground on a sunny day. There is nothing to be afraid of."

She starts to get annoyed (unmistakable red streaks) so I try another tack. "I know, I know, you're afraid of the *future*, what-*if* and all that. Can't you see that's imaginary? It's just your mind telling you a story about what bad things can happen. None of it exists."

She's looking at me like it is making some sense.

"Just come on the adventure," I say. "Stay in the *here* and *now* as we go, and I promise there won't be anything to be afraid of."

"How can you promise *that*?" she asks.

"Because there never is," I say.

She shakes her head and I know I've lost her. "How about this," I say. "Come on the adventure, and if you start to feel scared, ask yourself, 'What would I do if I weren't afraid?' and then do that, whatever it is. It'll be our question of the day. I promise, you'll have a blast."

She tips her head to the side. "You make it sound so easy," she says.

"It is easy," I say. "Will you try it?"

She doesn't have a chance to answer me before Dante starts barking orders.

"P.K., go take your tent down so you don't have to pay for a night while we're gone. Critter, come help me sort this gear." He is rummaging through a duffel bag in the back of his car.

I look into her eyes. "So, are we doing this?"

"Oh, all right," she says.

"Attagirl!" I wrap my arms around her and lift her up so

her feet leave the ground. Then I catch myself—oops, *way* too much affectionate enthusiasm—and set her back down. She seems to hold on to me for an extra beat, though. At least I *think* so.

While P.K. breaks down the tent, Dante and I lay out ropes, cams, hexes, nuts, offsets, tricams, TCUs, quickdraws, extra slings, cordelettes, extra biners, daisy chains, ascenders, aiders, prussiks, nut tools, etc. Dante leans in close and talks quietly. "Dog, I see you slept on the picnic table last night. Is she your girlfriend, or your friend, or what? I mean, is she *available*?"

Suddenly, out of the depths of my reptilian brain, a monster emerges—a very *male* monster, dripping testosterone from sharpened fangs, ready to rise up to my full height and rip the short, somewhat swarthy competition to shreds. "Dante," I say, firm and calm, "she is so *not* available."

FORTY-SEVEN

P.K.

I do not like how Dante looks at me. It's like his girlfriend breaks up with him one day, and his babe radar is up and running the very next morning. Well, no thank you, O self-absorbed one.

I bring my rack and rope over and drop them on the ground with the gear the guys are sorting. "Let's take my stuff and just add your extra cams and ascenders," I say. It's a political move. Using my gear will give me some decision-making power. Dante looks my rack over and approves. He's probably thinking he'd rather it be my gear than his, abandoned high on the cliff with the leaver biners if we can't make it to the top.

FORTY-EIGHT

CRITTER

We park at a pull-off on the loop road, stick the please-do-not-tow-our-car permit in the windshield, and start off across the Mojave Desert. The cliffs loom in the distance. They've got layers of pink, red, redder, and black. Aztec sandstone. The guidebook says they used to be sand dunes during the Jurassic period. I imagine a T. rex with shades: Surf's up!

Dante says we've got three hours of hiking and scrambling if we move fast. "This climb is so awesome," he tells me. "I've staked it out—it's probably eight or ten pitches, at least a thousand feet, pristine hard stuff, but I'm sure there're some moderate pitches, too. We'll swing leads. You'll love it!"

FORTY-NINE

P.K.

Single file through the desert, our hiking boots crunching on the rocky path. We wind among cactus, yucca, creosote bushes, and wildflowers in lavender, pink, and yellow. I smell the wild sage as I brush past it.

And here's Dante, jabbering on about the climb, planning it with Critter, as if I'm not here, as if I'm something they have to drag up after them like a haul bag. I hear Critter's voice in my head: *Ask yourself, "What would I do if I weren't afraid?" and then do that, whatever it is.*

"Hey, Dante," I call out. He's at the front of our line, I'm at the back.

He keeps talking and walking.

"Dante." I say it sharply.

"Huh? What?" He acts like I just woke him up or something.

"Stop being such a jerk," I say.

He stops walking.

I continue. "You think the guys do the first ascending and the girl, what, holds the belay rope? Makes the sandwiches? No. You want me along, I'm leading, too."

He's surprised, doesn't know what to say. For a moment I think he might just say, "Well, we don't want you along, then."

I mentally sift through my pack; what am I carrying that they can't do without? The peanut butter. I'll hold it hostage.

"Uh . . . yeah, fine." Dante blinks, as if this new idea—me leading on the first ascent—is causing a renaissance in his brain. "You can lead. There might be an easy five-six or five-seven section for you to try."

Before I can wind up again, Critter steps in. First, he snorts condescendingly, which is totally cool. Then he says, "Dante, hello? She leads five-eleven."

Dante shakes his head, then nods, then shakes his head again, so it looks like he's doing neck circles. "Wow. I mean, that's great. I mean, yeah, great. You've definitely got to lead."

We resume our single-file hike, *crunch, crunch, crunch.*

I smile to myself. Normally I would have been afraid to stick it to Dante and demand my place on the first-ascent team. I like Critter's question of the day.

FIFTY

CRITTER

You go, P.K. She put him in his place and shut him up in one short exchange. The quiet gives me a chance to consider my options. I mean, exactly how much trouble could I get into if I make a move on this girl? And if she lets me?

Police? If her parents hire, say, a private detective, it won't take him/her long to research the major climbing areas and find out where we are. (I'm sure lovely Melanie will be very helpful in that regard.) Is it statutory rape if we're both under eighteen? If it is, it'll just give *the* cops yet another reason to lead me away in shackles.

Angry parents? Maybe her mom and dad will come looking for her themselves, possibly in combination with a family vacation to the West. I can imagine the narration to their vacation slide show: "Here we are looking for P.K. in

Yosemite National Park. Those waterfalls were absolutely *stunning*. And here we are at Yellowstone. Did you know that geyser erupts like clockwork, every half hour? And here we are in Las Vegas. Honey, you do not look happy in this picture—he's still mad about how much money I lost in the slot machines. Oh, and here we are, reunited with P.K.! That's the Mojave Desert you see in the background. And there's that nasty Critter boy being led away in handcuffs. Did you know he was a mental patient? It's just awful. He brainwashed our little girl and kidnapped her and (*sniff*) had his way with her. We *are* pressing charges, you know. . . ."

Then there's Dante, with his if-you're-not-nailing-her-let-me-have-at-her attitude. He's definitely over eighteen—said he's done with school. So he'd get arrested big-time. Plus, I'd kill him, so there are a few downsides he might want to be aware of.

I stop walking and wait for P.K. to catch up. Her face is flushed and she's sweaty—the sun is high and hot by now.

"Water break?" I ask.

She nods.

"Hey, Dante, take ten. We're getting a drink," I call to him.

I pull out the drinking tube of my CamelBak, open the valve, and lean in close to her so she can get it into her mouth. We're so close I can smell the sunblock on her skin, feel her breath on my neck. She closes her eyes, wraps her lips around the tube, and sucks long and hard, gulping. When she opens her eyes, I'm staring, staring. I think my mouth is open and I'm breathing hard, too. Our eyes meet and lock for just an instant.

Then she laughs. "Don't look so desperate," she says. "Here." She sticks the tube into my mouth and steps away, fanning herself.

I drink and watch her. Suddenly, all my earlier thoughts seem ridiculous. First of all, this is not a girl who would do the deed with someone she met a few days ago. She's more of a *maybe*-after-a-year-in-a-committed-relationship kind of girl. And second of all, no matter how you cut it, when her parents catch up to us I'm going to be in insanely deep doo-doo. And that's not even considering the fact that my parents and the hospital have most assuredly sent *the* cops out after me.

FIFTY-ONE

P. K.

So now I've got Dante the wolf and Critter the puppy dog both making eyes at me. This should be interesting. I'll have no problem staying on top of the game, though. There's a reason why the girl is always the fox.

FIFTY-TWO

CRITTER

After a couple of hours, Dante leads us off the flat desert trail toward a canyon. Our hike turns into a scramble up steep scree, over boulders and ledges. Cliff walls rise on either side of us, and it's cooler here in their shade. The rocks are astounding colors: white with red polka dots, pink and red stripes, varnished black.

I take it all in as we go: a stream trickling by; scrubby, prickly-leaved bushes; an iridescent blue lizard scurrying out of my way. Squirrels chatter from gnarled oak trees. Probably haven't seen humans in a while.

We're moving fast and steadily on the steep terrain, breathing too hard for conversation. But soon my stomach starts to talk to me.

"Hey guys, you want to break for lunch?" I ask.

The response is immediate and positive: they both throw down their packs.

P.K. opens her pack and hauls out the peanut butter, bread, apples, and a knife, and lays it all on a flat rock. We splash water from the stream on our faces, necks, arms. As we share the knife and make our lunches, I strike up a hopefully innocuous nonclimbing conversation.

"So, Dante, are you named after Dante Alighieri, author of *The Divine Comedy* and all that?"

Dante takes a large bite of apple. "Hell, no," he says. "My mother was working at a bar called Dante's Inferno when she had me."

P.K. laughs, and in typical undiplomatic P.K. style, she asks, "Didn't your dad mind his son being named after a *bar*?"

Dante stares at her. I sense he has fought many a playground brawl over the issue of his father—or lack of one.

"Well, it just shows you shouldn't ever assume anything,

huh?" I say, hoping to diffuse the tension that could now easily be cut with our peanut-butter-smeared knife.

"What about you, Critter? Is your real name Christopher?" P.K. asks.

I shake my head. "I know, that's what everyone thinks, that I had a little brother or sister who couldn't say *Christopher* and called me Critter and it stuck. But it's not."

"So . . . what *is* your real name?" she asks.

I shrug. "It's Critter. My mom and dad were in a very earthy, crunchy phase when they had me, and decided that's what I was, a creature upon the earth. But since I was small, they decided *critter* was better than *creature*."

P.K. shakes her head slightly and puts on a polite smile. "Interesting," is all she says.

"Yeah, don't ever assume anything," Dante says to her in a mean way. The guy has got an edge to him. "I know I've got you pegged, though," he says, still looking at her. "You're a preacher's kid all the way."

"A *what*?" P.K. frowns.

"Your old man's a preacher, right? That's how you got your nickname."

Uh-oh, I think, *now he's going to make some comment about her being a prude.* It's the typical bad-boy challenge that they hope will get a modest girl to open up and show some sparks of wildness. I feel like throwing up my hands and shouting, "Don't do it!" but P.K. breaks in.

"My father is a tax accountant," she says coldly. Then, while giving him a stare that could freeze fire, she says, "Don't *ever* assume *anything*."

FIFTY-THREE

P. K.

Soon Dante will just be *in* his place, and I won't have to keep putting him there.

The scrambling seems to go on forever, but finally we reach an area where the cliff curves around us like a huge amphitheater and Dante stops and says, "This is it."

I look up. A crack system travels up the rock face, sometimes leaning right, sometimes disappearing and reappearing to the left higher up, traveling past several roofs, through sections where the rock is cream-colored, or pink as coral, then on to rock that is red as dried blood or sleek black.

"Wow." Critter breathes the word, as if he's in a cathedral.

"It must be at least a thousand feet," says Dante.

"It's gorgeous," I say. Then all I want is to have at it. "Let's *go*," I say.

We hike the last bit to the base of the climb, throw down our packs, and launch into action. Critter and I flake out the ropes, feeding them into neat piles, while Dante racks up (he actually *asked* if it was okay with us if he led the first pitch—the boy is learning).

Critter settles in to belay, and Dante starts up. He moves quickly, confidently, only putting in a few pieces of gear. His climbing is like his personality: bold.

"This part's easy, five-eight max," he calls to us.

I realize we'll need to write this all down, rate each pitch, describe it, give directions.

"Did you bring paper?" I call up to him.

"Look in my pack," says Dante.

I find a pen and paper, and begin to write. "Start at the obvious crack system near a large boulder."

Dante climbs to a ledge about 150 feet up. He builds a belay anchor and we hear him shout, "Off belay!"

"You want to second this pitch, maybe lead the next one?" Critter asks.

"Sure," I say.

I tie in to the rope. As I tighten the laces on my rock shoes, Critter watches me.

"Nice touch," he says, eyeing the strips of orange tape I've got wrapped around the lavender laces on my shoes.

"Oh, yeah," I say. "Everybody's got these shoes, so it helps to tell them apart." Dante pulls my rope taut. I call, "That's me."

Dante shouts, "Belay on."

I check my knot, check my harness, call, "Climbing," up to Dante, and when I hear, "Climb on," I take off.

It is wonderful to move over rock again. I feel the strength in my fingers, the sureness in my feet, the freedom in leaving the ground and joining the vertical world. The climbing isn't hard. As I go, I take out the gear Dante has put into the rock. All of his placements are solid. I reach the ledge easily and clip myself in to the belay anchor while making a mental note: excellent anchor. The guy might be a jerk, but he's got good skills.

I'm a little nervous about being with Dante on the belay ledge without Critter. "I agree, five-eight," I say, hoping to focus solely on the climbing.

"Do you concur?" he asks.

I laugh. He sounds like the doctor scene in the movie *Catch Me If You Can*. I loved that movie, too. "Yes, I concur."

"Critter, you're on belay," Dante shouts down.

While Critter climbs, we talk about the movie, and how it was a true story and that guy really did do all that impersonation stuff when he was a teenager. As soon as Critter is close enough, we start badgering him about if he concurs on the 5.8 rating. It feels good to have a running joke. Better than a running feud. The climbing has washed away the earlier tensions.

I start looking at the rock above us. This could be my lead. I can see the crack system for about forty feet, and it looks totally protectable with gear. But then there's a small roof, and I can't see beyond it. Is this one of the places where the crack disappears and makes placing gear impossible? It looked good from the ground, I decide. And I'm warmed up and psyched. I'll do it.

"I'll take the next pitch," I tell Dante.

"Go for it," he says.

"Mind if I take the gear off you now?" I ask.

"Oh, baby, you can have my equipment anytime you want it."

I roll my eyes, but refrain from starting another argument. I start pulling the gear off his harness and racking it on my harness, organizing it the way I want it. When Critter is safely on the belay ledge, he gives me the couple of pieces of gear I'd left in for him. I'm ready to go.

"I'll give her a catch," Critter says.

He must have read my mind. I'd much rather have my life in his hands than in Dante's.

I'm nervous and excited. My first time on virgin rock. My first time not knowing what lies ahead.

"Take a deep breath," Critter says.

Oh good, he'll be my coach as well as my belayer. I take a breath, blow it out slowly.

"You can do this," he says. "It's probably more five-eight. The crack is good; you've got all the gear you need."

I don't remind him that we can't see above the roof. I don't want to remind myself of that.

We go through the classic commands and it is comforting.

Me: On belay?

Critter: Belay on.

Me: Climbing.

Critter: Climb on.

I climb up a few moves, look at the crack, see what it needs: number-two Camalot. I pull the piece off my harness, slot it in. Perfect. I love it when my brain works right, sees the crack, knows the right piece on the first try. I snap on a quickdraw, clip the rope into the carabiner, and go. I move up ten feet, look again: number-twelve nut. Perfect. No one can say I'm bold with my gear—placing a piece every seven to ten feet suits me well. That way my falls will never be more than about twenty feet long.

Critter was right, it feels like more 5.8 climbing. Piece of cake. About sixty feet up I reach the roof. The crack splits it right up the middle. I slot a hex. The piece is high, over my head, so I pull up rope, hold it in my teeth, pull up more rope, then slide the rope into the biner. The biner shuts with a satisfying snap, Critter takes in the slack, and I'm well protected to attempt the roof.

I inch my feet up under the roof, reach over the top, feeling blindly for a hold. Got one. I kick one foot up, pull hard, and haul myself up and over.

There are cheers from down below.

"Nice!" calls Critter.

"Love the way you stuck out your butt," says Dante.

"That was five-nine, maybe harder!" I shout down to them.

"We'll let you know if we concur," Dante shouts back.

I'm standing on a large ledge. I assess the wall in front of me. It's pink, and it actually has red stripes running horizontally across it. Beautiful. A breeze cools my neck. But . . . where's the crack? I run my hand along the features. What used to be the crack has now become nothing more than a diagonal crease in the rock. From down below it looked like a crack. But there is nowhere to put gear. No way to build a belay anchor and bring the guys up.

Fear wells up in me. To get out of this I would have to *down*-climb that difficult roof—a scary proposition. It's always much harder to climb down than to climb up. And I'd lose face, maybe lose the guys' respect. And I'd lose trust in myself.

I look up. It's a face climb—thin, but decent holds. It's what I'm good at. I've got strong fingers, awesome balance. On top rope I wouldn't think twice about it. And that crease has got to turn into a crack again somewhere up there. Critter's question comes floating to me on the breeze: *What would I do if I weren't afraid?*

I take a deep, slow breath. "Critter, you got me?" I shout down.

"I've got you, girl."

I step out onto the face. My feet are confident. My fingers grip tiny holds as I feel my body flow up the rock. I am a dancer; the rock is my partner.

A part of my brain is giving me readouts: *Now your fall is twenty feet long . . . thirty feet . . . thirty-five feet . . . forty feet long.* But the part of me that is separate from the fear is calm, knows only the movement. It knows only joy. Critter was right; I am having a blast. Just as the readout is telling me I'm looking at a fifty-foot fall and serious injuries, I see it above my head: the crack has opened up again. Number-three cam. *Yes.* I get a good stance, a good hold with my left hand, and reach for the cam on my harness with my right hand. I fumble for it. The carabiner catches on my harness loop. Oh *God*, if I drop it I'm screwed.

Suddenly fear is there, full-blown and real. There is a huge roof below me; I will *hit* it if I fall. I will bounce down, breaking bones and smashing body parts. I will hang there, bloodied and half dead until they are able to lower me. The first ascent will be over. They'll have to carry me out. Even if I'm dead, they'll have to carry me out.

My hands shake. My feet vibrate up and down on their holds—sewing-machine legs. Slot the piece, *now*! I lift the cam high, toward the crack. I can barely retract the trigger; my strength is leaving me, sabotaged by fear. I shove the cam into the crack. It's good. I grasp the rope with my right hand, pull it up, hold it with my teeth, pull again. I lift the rope toward the carabiner on the cam. I'm shaking, fumbling. I miss the clip. I drop the rope; the weight of it nearly pitches me off. I scream and slap my right hand onto a hold.

FIFTY-FOUR

CRITTER

When P.K. first begins the pitch, Dante is in full drooling mode, and as soon as she's out of earshot he starts in. "*Cute* butt. Oh man, I love it when she stems."

I ignore him. Or at least I don't say anything. I do agree with him, though—very cute butt. Still, I concentrate more on the belay: not too tight, no extra slack, shoot out rope when she pulls it up to clip, listen for the clip, then pull it back in. She's climbing great, looking solid. And she's finding good gear placements.

The roof looks like a challenge, but she does it in style. When we can't see her anymore, Dante says, "Show over," and turns to look at the view.

The rope is still for a few moments, then P.K. asks if I've got her, as if she's about to try something hard. After that, the rope feeds out smooth and slow. There are no I'm-putting-in-a-piece-of-gear-now stops, and no I'm-clipping-now yanks. Just even, consistent feeding-out.

"There's no gear up there," I say to Dante.

He looks up, but we still can't see her—that roof is too big. "Not good," he says as he watches the rope feed out. Then, more brightly, "Maybe it's five-three and she's just cruising."

"Maybe," I say. "But then why would she have asked me if I had her?"

We are both silent, tense, waiting. Finally, the rope stops.

"I think she found a placement," I say.

"Or a place too hard to climb," Dante says.

Then, thank God, there is the yank. I shoot out rope. A second yank. *Clip it*, I send my will up to her.

Suddenly the rope goes slack. We hear her scream.

"Oh no. She missed the clip," I say.

"Come on, P.K., *do* it," Dante says. He is sending her his will, too.

FIFTY-FIVE

P.K.

Full-blown panic. I can hardly breathe. *What would I do if I weren't afraid?*

For a moment I'm furious. That's the question that got me into this mess. But I also know it's my only way out. I rest my helmet against the rock. *What would I do if I weren't afraid?* I would reach down, pull up the rope, and clip it into the biner. The only thing that can hurt me now—maybe even kill me—is fear. I need to clip that piece. Keep fear out, and I'm home free.

Gingerly, I let go with my left hand and shake out my arm, giving my cramped muscles a break. Better. Then I get the good hold again, reach for the rope with my right hand again, use my teeth again, pull up more rope, reach it to the biner—stay calm—and make my fingers slip the rope into the biner. The biner snaps shut. The rope is where it should be. I let out my relief in a loud, wordless shout to the wind and rocks and sky. I am safe.

FIFTY-SIX

CRITTER

I pull the slack back in and wait. There it is again: the yank. I shoot out rope. We are silent. Then, faint and far away, we hear it: *snap.*

"I think she got it," I say.

The next thing we hear is P.K.'s voice in a victory yell.

"Yeah, she got it," says Dante, smiling.

A short time later we hear her shout, "Off belay!" I let out my breath. I didn't even realize I was holding it. P.K. pulls my rope taut and calls down, "Critter, you're on belay. Climb when ready."

I unclip from the anchor and stretch a bit to let go of the tension. Then I call, "Climbing," up to P.K. and slide my hands into the crack. Rock. It's one of the absolutely coolest parts of the illusion—ancient, unyielding, alive in that sneaky way that is particular to things that are generally believed to be unconscious. I feel that aliveness as I move up the rock face. I get to the roof and hoist myself over it. "It's at least five-nine," I call down to Dante. Then I look at the wall in front of me. It's a blank face. No crack, no gear, small holds. I move up and right, toward where P.K. is on a ledge high above. It's hard—*way* hard. It makes me shaky inside to realize P.K. did this with no protection. It's as if I feel her fear.

"Nice lead," I say when I get close to her.

She shakes her head and rolls her eyes, which I gather is all she wants to say about it right now.

I join her on the ledge and get clipped into the anchor. I've trailed Dante's rope. P.K. puts his rope into her belay device and lets Dante know he's on belay. It's a tiny ledge we're on. I use that as an excuse to sit very close to her, our thighs touching. Ah, the climbing ledge: one of Cupid's weapons for erasing personal space.

Shortly, we see Dante come up over the roof. "Five-nine, I concur," he calls to us. Then he surveys the wall in front of him. "I *hate* thin-face climbing," he whines.

"You're on top rope. Stop complaining," P.K. tells him.

Dante starts up slowly, almost hesitantly—very different from the grab-and-haul-butt style he uses when there are overhangs and bigger holds around.

Suddenly we hear a stream of expletives as Dante falls.

"Dante, you're kidding me," P.K. chides him as she holds the rope taut with her brake hand. "It's *not* that hard.

"Typical macho guy," P.K. says to me. "Give him a five-thirteen overhang and he's fine, but put him on a five-eight face and he doesn't know what to do."

"Uh, P.K.," I say, "I don't think that face is five-eight, I think—"

But I am interrupted by another round of expletives from below. "My God, P.K. How did you do this?" Dante dangles, rubbing his forearms. He gets back on the rock and tries the move again. He falls again. More expletives.

"It was easy," P.K. says quietly, mostly to herself. "That was the easy part, the part where I wasn't afraid. . . ."

She's looking rattled. Just as a precaution I take hold of the brake strand of the rope to back up her belay.

"You've got to use your feet there, Dante," I tell him. "Trust them—the rock is gritty, your feet'll stick."

Dante tries again and again, but keeps falling. Finally, he grabs the rope and hauls himself up a few feet to where there are better holds.

When he reaches the ledge, he squeezes in between us, exhausted and sweaty. "I'd give it five-eleven-c or -eleven-d because that's my limit on face climbing. Do you concur?" he asks.

I nod. "Yep. Definitely hard five-eleven. What do you think, P.K.?"

One look at her tells me all I need to know. "I think if she tries to concur it'll make her puke," I say. "Let's change the subject and figure out what we're doing—up or down?"

We take stock of our situation: the sinking sun and the number of climbers on our team who are about to puke, and decide to fix the rope to the anchor, rappel, and come back to finish the route tomorrow.

FIFTY-SEVEN

P.K.

Oh God, what did I do? I almost killed myself, or messed myself up royally. 5.11c or d—what was I *thinking*? Actually, that was the thing—I wasn't thinking. I was flowing, not scared a bit, just in the moment, in the movement.

I feel sick. Dante is cooking some stuff that looked like dried mice when he took it out of the package, but he promises it will taste good once he adds water and heats it up. But I don't think I can eat. I keep thinking how horrible it would have been for my parents, getting the call that I'd died, or that I was in the hospital and would never walk again, or was brain-damaged—

"P.K.!" Critter jolts me out of my terrifying thoughts.

"What?" I demand. Why is he yelling at me when I'm clearly upset?

"Stop it," he says sternly.

I wasn't doing anything, just sitting here. "Stop what?"

"Stop thinking about all the bad stuff that didn't happen."

I shake my head slightly. "How did you know?"

"Because you're thinking really loud, okay?" He seems annoyed, or maybe it's embarrassed. "You're creating a horrible story, with demons and dragons in it, and you're scaring yourself silly. Can't you see it's all made-up? It's a *story*. It's only in your head. It's *not real*."

"But what if I had fallen?" I demand. I'm close to tears. "Then it wouldn't be just a story."

"P.K." He is exasperated. "You didn't fall. It's over. There-fore it follows the Law of Inevitability. There is a zero percent chance of you falling."

For a moment, all the fear drains out of me, and an im-mense calm seeps in. He's right. It's over. I'm absolutely fine. The bad stuff is only in my imagination. But then, it's as if fear is sitting in the third row and it raises its hand to make a comment. *People do fall, you know*, it says. "But Critter, some people fall, and die or get messed up," I say.

He nods. "And some people are in car accidents or are killed by suicide bombers. That's their adventure, and some-day it may be yours, but not *now*, not today. Your adventure right now is to eat some of these rehydrated mice Dante has made for us."

I hold my stomach and groan.

"It's not mice." Dante defends his cooking. "The package said something about chicken."

And actually, it does smell good. I am suddenly raven-ous.

Critter leans in to me and says, "Remember, take the ham-ster off"—he pantomimes picking up a hamster and moving it—"the treadmill."

I hold my head in my hands. "Oh God, rodents in my head, rodents in my dinner . . ."

"All right, fine," says Dante. "You think it's mice, I'll eat it all."

"No!"

FIFTY-EIGHT

CRITTER

I couldn't exactly have said, "Because there's a cauldron of slate-gray/black fear colors boiling around your body." And I sure as hell can't tell her what I did and why I can see the colors.

After we eat, P.K. and Dante take the dishes to the creek to wash them while I organize our gear for tomorrow. They're talking and laughing—you'd never know they'd been at each other's throats a few hours ago. Dante has been pimping: serving P.K. her stew, going on about what an amazing climber she is, what an impressive lead she did. The testosterone monster is slowly uncoiling itself inside me.

I look up to see Dante playfully bump P.K.'s hip with his hip. Then, ohmigod she bumps him back.

The monster springs.

"*Hey*, P.K.!" I shout.

She turns. "What?" she asks.

I have no idea what to say, other than, *Stop flirting with him!*

"Uh . . . do you know what happened to the extra number-two cam?" I ask lamely.

"Yeah, duh, we left it in one of the anchors the ropes are attached to," she says.

"Oh. Right. You guys need any help over there?" I ask.

"I don't need any help at all," Dante answers. And then he makes the mistake of sliding his arm around the small of P.K.'s back and drawing her close to him. I've never seen a girl shove so hard. *Bam*—he's on his butt on the ground.

"Am I wearing a sign, 'Open for Business'?" she snaps.

"Chill out," Dante says. He picks himself up and goes off to sulk.

I look down and grin. The monster lays its head back down and closes its eyes. But it is definitely still awake.

FIFTY-NINE

P.K.

The moon rises and shines down from the swath of sky above our canyon. Its light is crystal clear. Every rock, every tree branch casts a sharp shadow.

I am tired, body, soul, and mind. Dante takes his sleeping bag and beds down on the one flat space there is available. There's no way I'm bedding down near him.

Critter seems to read my mind—again. "Let's scramble down a ways," he says. "I saw another flat area on our way up here."

He carries my sleeping bag and sleeping pad, and we find another good spot. As I'm laying my stuff out, I realize he is planning on leaving me here alone, giving me my space again like he did last night. But him I can trust. His company, weird as he is sometimes, I would enjoy.

He hovers. He doesn't really want to leave. How can I ask

him to sleep with me—next to me—without it sounding like a come-on?

I am saved by a coyote. He, or she, sets up a howl so eerie, so ghostly, that Critter and I stare at each other, wide-eyed.

"Scary," I say, even though I think it is beautiful.

He hesitates. Then, finally, he pops the question. "You want some company?"

"Definitely," I say, trying not to sound too eager. "Go get your sleeping bag," I add, in case he thinks I just want him to sit with me awhile.

The night is magical. It is as if there is life in the breeze, the moonlight, the cliffs that tower on either side of us. Critter comes back with his sleeping gear and lays it down next to mine, not too close. I think, *He's being such a gentleman.* Then, suddenly, I am seized by an awful thought: what if he doesn't like me? I mean, he's stuck with me, but that doesn't mean he wants to be. Dante has been falling all over himself with the come-ons, but Critter has kept his distance. No flirting, no using the chill in the air last night as an excuse to share the tent, even after I told him he could. He probably only ended up on my lap in the truck by accident in his sleep. I probably imagined him making moony eyes at me while we shared a drink from his CamelBak. I feel deflated, embarrassed. And the magic has gone out of the desert night.

SIXTY

CRITTER

Oh man, what's this? P.K.'s colors were her usual peach with some gorgeous streaks of silver, and they just crumpled into this awful mustard-yellow. What in the world is she thinking about now?

She gets into her sleeping bag and zips it up. I could have sworn she seemed interested in hanging out together, but now she's doing a silent I'm-going-to-sleep-immediately routine.

I get into my bag and zip it, too. I hope I didn't lay it down too close to hers.

I prop myself up on one elbow and look at her. She's lying on her back with her eyes closed.

"You shouldn't go to sleep thinking bad thoughts," I say.

She frowns and opens her eyes. "I wasn't doing the scary-death-scenario thing," she says.

"I know. You were . . . I don't know what you're doing, but it's not good."

She shifts onto her side toward me and props her head on her arm. "Critter, how do you do that?" she asks. "How do you always know what I'm thinking?" She sounds sort of annoyed and sort of amazed.

"I don't know exactly what you're thinking, I just know . . ." I trail off. I can't tell her about the colors. I feel myself begin to close down, to protect the things I believe would freak her out.

There is a sudden wind in the canyon. It scatters dry oak

leaves and kicks up dust. It also reminds me that I have been thinking too small: one girl, one hamster on a wheel going round and round. I lie back, look up at the moon glowing like a pearl, feel the dark majesty of the cliffs, feel myself expanding to take it all in, to become part of it. The lone coyote sets up its howl. P.K. and I look at each other.

What would I do if I weren't afraid?

I reach over, touch the side of her face. Her eyes are on me. She doesn't flinch away.

What would I do if I weren't afraid?

I lean in, touch my lips to hers, lightly, like a question. Her answer is yes. I kiss her gently, slide my hand behind her neck, kiss her more deeply.

A current runs through my body—our kiss, our bodies, the moon, the wind, the canyon, it is all made of the same living, pulsing, vibrant light. It runs through me and through her, and between us and all around us. There is no separation. And I could tell her anything.

SIXTY-ONE

P.K.

Oh. My. God.

I didn't know anybody could be such a good kisser.

When Critter pulls back, he looks at me. I'm totally breathless, but I try to hide it. I don't want him suggesting we throw off our sleeping bags and clothes and all. But he just smiles, scooches over close to me, and tosses his arm across my chest.

"Good night," he says.

I'm so surprised, I laugh out loud.

He lifts his head up. "What's funny?" he asks.

I shrug. "I guess that you didn't keep kissing me and keep pushing for more until I said no."

He looks concerned. "Did you want me to?"

I laugh again. "No. It's just what I'm used to, that's all."

He lies back down and gives me a squeeze with the arm he's got draped over me. And that's it. No more talking, no more kissing.

I watch the stars for a few minutes, marveling at what a very odd person Critter is. But then my eyes blur with sleep, and as I begin to fade, the words come to me, what I would have said to him if we'd kept talking: *It was absolutely perfect.*

SIXTY-TWO

CRITTER

Morning. I can tell the sun is up because the sky is a deep, clear blue, though our canyon is in cold shadows. P.K. is still asleep. I hope she appreciates what a heroic effort it took for me not to jump her last night.

I hike up to where our packs are. Heat. I get the stove going for hot water. Coffee and oatmeal—whoever invented instant should be given the Nobel Prize.

Before long the other two are up, yawning, finding their bowls and mugs. Our dish sponge is gone, and there's some kind of small-animal poop scattered on the rocks where it used to be.

"Huh," says Dante. "I didn't know moldy dish sponges were such a hot item among the night-creature crowd."

P.K. stamps her feet and rubs her arms, trying to warm up. I do the only decent thing: I envelop her in a warm hug and stand there seeping body heat into her. She seems to melt into me. *Very* nice.

"I see somebody got it on last night," Dante says, leering.

I let go of P.K. so Dante's comments don't embarrass her. "Better?" I ask.

"Yep," she says, and goes for the hot water.

"Everybody got their ascenders ready?" I ask brightly, figuring we need a new subject.

Now both of them glare at me. "Hey," I say, "it's not my fault we get to start the day jugging."

We eat breakfast, make peanut butter sandwiches, and cram them into the zippered pouches on our CamelBaks. Then we treat some water from the creek to fill the Camel-Baks. We'll try to finish the route today before dark.

With gear clanking on our harnesses we scramble to where our ropes hang, one above the other—a straight line up to where we stopped climbing yesterday. We look up. It's kind of like doing the rope climb in gym class, albeit with the help of ascenders, but for three hundred feet.

"I'll go first," I say. I seem to be the most psyched for the climb—probably because I'm first up to lead.

I connect a pair of ascenders and aiders to the rope, clip myself in with my daisy chains, and slip my feet into the aiders. I slide the ascenders up and stand up in the aiders, then it's slide, stand, slide, stand, pushing my weight up the rope. It's still easier than reclimbing the 5.11c face, but *man*, it's hard. I sing the "Bulgarian Boat Song," keeping time with my hauling: "Yo-o, heave, ho, oh yo-o, heave, ho . . ."

"Critter, that makes it sound even worse!" P.K. whines.

"Yeah, man, give us a break," says Dante. "Can't you sing 'Stairway to Heaven' or something?"

I start in, "And I'm cli-i-mbing a stai-i-rway to hea-a-ven," but soon I'm too out of breath to sing anything.

At the top of the first rope I clip into the anchor, remove my ascenders, and shout, "Off rope!" so they know the next person can start up. I catch my breath as I hook in to the next rope. Then I sing the theme song from *Gilligan's Island* to the tune of "Stairway to Heaven," which fits perfectly.

SIXTY-THREE

P.K.

Can't stop thinking about kissing Critter last night. I keep ending up with a silly grin on my face. Need to make sure Dante doesn't see or he'll know why I'm grinning—or think he knows—and harass me about it.

When we're finally all gathered on the top ledge (least fun thing about putting in a new route: jugging), it's time to fo-

cus. No more kissing fantasies. Critter is leading and I'm belaying. His life is in my hands.

SIXTY-FOUR

CRITTER

Gear: check.

Chalk bag: check.

Harness on correctly after taking a piss that floated away
in a spray: check.

Brain: check.

Conversation before I start up:

Dante: Are you ready, man? Virgin rock. It's just like
nailing a girl who's never done it before.

P.K.: Shut *up*.

Me: No fighting while I'm gone, you two.

P.K.: Belay on.

Me: Climbing.

P.K.: Climb on.

I step out onto the wall, move up, slot a hex. Solid. I slap on a
quickdraw, clip in the rope, keep moving. The rock is warm
under my hands. *No one has ever touched this before. . . .*

The crack runs up and slightly left. It eats gear. I feel the fluid motion in my body as I jam, crimp, and high-step my way up thirty feet, forty feet, fifty feet.

Comments from the peanut gallery below:

Dante: She's looking right at your butt. I think she likes it.

P.K.: Dante, give it a rest. Critter, you're looking good up there.

Dante: See what I mean?

I move up higher and the comments stop, or I just can't hear them anymore. The world fades away. There is nothing but me moving, placing pieces, clipping in the rope. The rock is solid under my toes and fingers, this massive cliff that is allowing me to make my way. The crack thins. I place a number-three nut, then a .5 TCU—small gear. The crack disappears. Now there is only me moving, still fluid, still reaching, pulling, stepping, shifting. The holds are thinning. The rock is in my face, overhanging. Forearms begin to pump. Still moving up, still reaching. Can't hold on. Fingers slip.

"Falling!"

The *drop*. Wind whooshing in my ears, rock going by in a blur. Then the *stop*, in which I wish that my harness and my balls had more space between them.

P.K.: Critter, you okay?

Dante: That was a forty-foot whipper! You got *balls*.

Me (*shifting uncomfortably as I dangle in my harness*): I know. Yeah, I'm (*squirm, shift*) fine.

I look up and remember the last piece I placed.

Me: Oh man. I fell on a point-five TCU.

Dante: Well, it held.

Me: Thanks, P.K. Nice catch.

P.K.: I'm just glad it was a clean fall and you didn't hit anything.

SIXTY-FIVE

P.K.

Okay, so I was looking at his butt. But when someone is right above you, what else is there to look at?

Then he's up there running it out, going waaaay above his last piece of gear. Suddenly he pops. I lock off the belay. He's airborne, long blond ponytail flying, arms and legs bent like a pouncing cat. There's a jolt on the rope when he stops.

He's not rattled. He's not freaked. All he does is shake out his arms to get rid of the forearm pump, and go on up the wall again. He backs up the .5 TCU with another piece, and then he falls *three more times*. He's climbing a little farther eac me, still with no gear, so the last time he falls it's at least fifty feet. He hits his hip on the wall when he stops, and is going "Ow, ow, *ow*!" Dante is calling him the Flying Monkey, and I'm thinking, *For the love of God, let's bail.* But Critter says, "I'm so close! It looks like there's a gear placement just above where I fell this time. I'm working it out. I'll get it."

All I can do is belay him back up and be ready to catch another heinous fall.

"That rope is toast," says Dante. "He owes me a new rope after all those falls."

"I don't hear you offering to take over the lead," I shoot back. That shuts him up. Critter and I don't have the cash to go buying Dante a new rope.

Critter moves up the rock, past where he fell the first time, past where he fell the second time, and the third time. . . . He makes it to the crack. He reaches for gear, pulls a cam off his harness, places it. Then in one fluid motion, he pulls the rope up and clips in.

I am relieved, and more than a little bit jealous. Why couldn't *I* be that calm thirty feet above my last piece of gear?

SIXTY-SIX

CRITTER

Trying and Flying 101 course description: After the first time you fall, *don't think about it!*

P.K. and Dante concur on the 5.12a difficulty rating (they both fall numerous times, and Dante needs a rope boost). They also concur on the R protection rating, as in, "The leader will probably get injured if he/she falls" (though it's not serious, we decide that the grapefruit-sized hematoma forming on my left hip counts as an injury).

Dante leads the next pitch, which includes a huge roof with a crack running right through the center. We concur on 5.11b.

After that the rock backs off, the pitches get easier (5.9, 5.7, and 5.5), and we sail to the top in high spirits. When we reach the summit we yell and scream and high-five each other and throw half-eaten peanut butter sandwiches off the cliff in celebration. We even have a momentary group hug, until we realize we smell much too bad to be doing that kind of thing.

Dante pumps his fists into the air and shouts, "First free ascent! Dante Tumilow, Critter, and P.K. whatever your last names are, five-twelve-a!" He rubs his hands together. "Now we've got to name it," he says, beaming. "How about Titanium Balls? Or maybe The Wong Way?"

P.K. groans. "Can we please think beyond penis and scrotum names?"

Dante nods. "Sure. This is Vegas, so we can go more with the Tits-and-Beer kind of name."

P.K. groans louder.

The way back to our camp is a rocky scramble down a gully on the back side of the cliff. As we make our way down, P.K. and Dante argue. Dante defends his less-than-politically-correct name choices by bringing up other similarly titled climbs. "What about Bikini Whale and Wet T-shirt Night at Joshua Tree? Or how about Penis Colada at the Gunks? Hey, Critter you're a Gunks climber, don't they have—"

"Don't bring me into this," I say quickly. There are route names at the Gunks that would make P.K.'s dreads stand on end.

P.K. insists that the first ascent teams on all those climbs probably didn't have a female on them to keep the guys from giving them stupid names, and she says she won't stand for a male-chauvinist-pig title for our climb. Then she starts suggesting names like Jock Itch and Hung Like a Gerbil just to annoy Dante.

Finally, I interrupt them. "How about we think of each pitch and talk about what was on it. Maybe that'll give us some ideas."

They seem bored with my suggestion, but they do it.

Dante: First pitch, jam crack to a dihedral, small overhang, yada yada, five-eight.

P.K.: Second pitch, we said five-eleven-c, right? Geez, could have used a bolt on that one. Hand crack to the roof, then thin face back to finger crack.

Me: Third pitch. Twelve-a. Definitely could have used a bolt—or three. Let's see, left-leaning ramp to overhanging—

Dante: That's *it*.

Me: What's what?

Dante: That's the name. Could Have Used a Bolt.

P.K.: *Yes*.

Me: Perfect.

SIXTY-SEVEN

P.K.

By the time we get back to our packs, I'm so sweaty, grimy, and smelly all I can think of is water. I throw off my gear, find a small pool in the creek, and wallow in it with all my clothes on.

"There goes our drinking water," says Dante.

"Shut up. Go upstream if you need a drink," I say.

We didn't bring any soap—the area is too fragile for us to be messing it up with soap—but I scour myself with sand from the creek bed, rinse off, and feel refreshed. When I rejoin the guys at our camp they're whispering to each other. When they see me they clam up.

"You're talking about me," I say accusingly.

They are silent.

"So you're not even going to try to deny it? Are you saying what a pain I am for not letting you guys name the climb The Whores of Vegas or something?"

Critter shakes his head. "It's not that at all," he says.

They both just look at me.

"What?" I say. "What is it, then?"

Critter clears his throat. "I just was telling Dante I think the route needs an X rating . . . because of the pitch you led. Because of the runout above the roof."

My stomach does a little flip. I'd been trying not to think about it. X as in "A falling leader will probably suffer severe injuries and/or death." *Don't think about it.*

I nod slowly. "All right."

"Come on, it's our turn to cook," Critter says.

He keeps me busy fetching water, tasting the pasta sauce, and listening to stories about climbing at the Gunks. By the time dinner is ready, my clothes have dried right on me in the desert air, and my mind, instead of focusing backward on what could have happened on that X-rated climb, is happy in the moment, though it is doing a few furtive peeks at what could happen tonight when Critter and I lie down next to each other in the moonlight again.

SIXTY-EIGHT

CRITTER

The age-old second-night-at-the-campsite dilemma:

1. Do we pick up where we left off; start by making out and go further?
2. Do I keep it innocent, show her respect, and just kiss her good night again?
3. Do I completely leave her alone because I smell so bad?

I am momentarily saved from making a decision by the fact that after Dante beds down, and before we go to our sleeping bags, P.K. wants to sit on a rock and talk.

Conversation on the rock:

P.K.: You seemed so calm up there, even when you kept falling. How do you do that?

Me: It's easy. Don't think about the past, don't think about the future. There's never any fear in the present.

P.K.: Oh yeah? What if you're being chased by a grizzly bear?

Me: That's fear of the future, of being caught by the bear. What if he catches you and just looks at you? Then see, there was nothing to be afraid of.

P.K.: Not likely. What if he catches you and crunches your leg?

Me: That's not fear, that's pain. You deal with that in the present, too.

P.K.: What if he eats you?

Me (*shrugging*): Then you die.

P.K.: So, duh. *That's* something to be afraid of.

Me: Ha! That's the biggest lie of all. Dying is . . . it's pretty much the coolest thing I've ever done.

She raises her eyebrows at me and seems to stiffen. I start backpedaling, or at least it's an attempt at backpedaling that is more like diving deeper and deeper into muck.

Me: Not like it was cool like I'd try it again. I mean, it was a mistake to try it in the first place, really not a good idea, and not considerate toward my parents or my little sister, but once I was there, I found out it's not a bad thing to go through at all. In fact, it's completely awesome and amazing, and I learned things I never knew, like about what we're doing here and what our bodies are made of and stuff

like that, and so in a way it was a good thing it happened because otherwise I never would have figured things out and
I would have stayed all depressed and miserable and hating
life. But I'd never ever recommend it for someone who's depressed, you know, like I'd never say, "Oh, just flatline it for
a while and you'll have a different perspective." No, I still
think it was a dumb idea, and *way* too risky, and not exactly
a piece of cake trying to convince everyone that you're more
normal than ever when you come back from it all with ideas
they think are crazy. You know?

She shakes her head. She is a perfect example of what is
meant by the word *dumbfounded*. I realize there was a fourth
second-night-at-the-campsite possibility: go to sleep without
saying another word because you just royally freaked the girl
out by confessing that you tried to off yourself.

SIXTY-NINE

P.K.

Surprising? Yes. But then, Critter is often surprising. Shock-
ing? Not really, but he seems to think he has shocked me. He
clams up, goes to get his sleeping bag, and walks back past
me with it like he's going to find his own spot to sleep. I catch
his hand on the way by.

"Critter, it's not that bad," I tell him. "Lots of kids feel like
life is too hard, and they don't want to go on and they just
want to end it all."

He looks at me hopefully. "So you're not totally freaked out?"

I shake my head. "Nope."

He grins. "So . . . you want to make out?"

I laugh, and turn on the coy. "Maybe."

He puts his arm around me, then thinks better of it.

"Yeah," I say, fanning my nose. "You might want to keep the arms *down*."

"I should have joined you in the creek," he says. He lays his sleeping bag down on the rock so we can sit on it.

"So, did your parents finally come around to thinking you were normal again?" I ask.

He looks up at the night sky. "No," he says simply.

"Well, that's weird," I say. "What do they do, treat you like they have to walk on eggshells or something, like they're afraid you'll do something crazy again?"

He gives me a mischievous look. I can see he has no intention of continuing this conversation. "You did say, 'Maybe,' right?" he asks. "So that means I have to find out." He brushes my jaw with his fingertips and kisses me lightly. I feel the rush and tingle just like last night. He kisses me again. No more talking. I pull him toward me. I am lost in it.

Just when my body is starting to want more, just when my brain is saying, *Have some self-respect, girl—this is way too early in a relationship to be getting more body parts involved*, he slows up, gives me one more light kiss, pulls back, and looks at me.

"Time to get some sleep?" he asks.

I shrug, shake my head, then nod. Talk about mixed messages. "Uh . . . sure," I say.

We lay out our sleeping bags next to each other and zip ourselves into them. Then Critter comes all the way over so that he's got one leg and one arm draped over me. "Don't worry," he says. "There are two layers of one hundred percent down-filled breathable microfiber between us."

I like the feeling of his weight on me, his breath on my cheek. The moon is gone now, set behind the canyon wall. The stars glitter like a million diamonds in an ink-black sky. I lift one of my arms up so that my hand is silhouetted against the stars.

"Critter, what are our bodies made of?" I ask. "You said you learned."

He looks up at the stars and my hand. "Light," he says. "Swirling, orbiting light."

SEVENTY

CRITTER

History in the making:

> A. We have put in a new route, from the ground up, in the way of the old traditionalist climbers.
> B. I told P.K. more than I've told anyone about

what happened last winter (except my parents, and that ended badly).

C. I now hold the world's record in level of sexual arousal while saying, "Time to get some sleep?"

The historical theme continues the next day. After breakfast, Dante says we might as well do some more climbing, on an established route, before we go back. P.K. says she wants to do a classic trad climb. She looks through the guidebook and finds Swing Shift, a seven-pitch 5.10.

"Look at this," she says excitedly. "The first ascent was done by a teenager, this guy Joe Herbst from Las Vegas. It says he and Mark Moore did it in spring of 1977. *Cool.*"

We follow in the footsteps of our fellow teenager and climb Swing Shift. It's so different now, being on a climb that's all explained for us with directions and ratings. Kind of a metaphor for life: do you follow a path laid out for you by someone else so you always know what to expect, or do you strike off on your own into the unknown?

The climb is an awesome combination of finger crack, face, overhang, chimney, and corner climbing. We finish with plenty of daylight left. The descent is a series of rappels and we make it down by sunset.

"We've got to hoof it to the car," says Dante. "The permit was only for two nights."

Maybe it's the fast hiking. Maybe it's the general high

of climbing. Or maybe it's the high of getting to know P.K. and *really* liking her. Maybe it's just the quiet beauty of the desert as it settles down after a day of blazing sun, so that I'm busy noticing wildflowers closing up for the night and insects buzzing sleepily. Whatever it is, it keeps me from being alert, keeps me from paying attention to the car parked near ours in the pull-off, keeps me from looking in the windows of the car to make sure it's just empty, or a bunch of climbers or kids out drinking or whatever. It keeps me from grabbing P.K. and yelling, "Run!" when the two men step out of the car and walk toward us. It keeps me eerily calm as they say our names and tell us that Dante is free to go but P.K. and I will be coming with them. It keeps me feeling separate, as if I'm watching it all happen to someone else as Dante says, "Not good," and P.K. starts crying and they tell us to get into the backseat of the unmarked police car.

SEVENTY-ONE

Conversation in police car:

P.K. (*whispering, between sobs*): Oh God, Critter. They're going to handcuff us and separate us and lock us up. I've seen it on *Juvies* on TV.

Critter (*also whispering, his arm around P.K.*): Don't panic. Try to stay in the present with it, okay? You're in a car. We're together. No handcuffs yet—okay?

Officer from front seat: Whew, what's that smell?

Critter: That would be me, sir.

Officer (*turning up the AC*): All right, don't worry, we're taking you to a place where you can get a shower.

P.K. (*in a squeaking whisper*): See? They're taking us to one of those . . . those lock-up places where people get raped in the shower!

Critter (*holding her tighter, trying to calm her down*): P.K., come back to *now*. You're doing the scary-scenario thing again. Right now you're fine. Think about it—do you have a problem now? Right this second?

P.K.: Yes.

Critter: What's the problem?

P.K.: I'm *scared*!

Critter: You're scared of the future. Take a deep breath— okay, turn your face away from me and take a deep breath— and look at where you are *now*. Is there anything to be afraid of? Not what's in your mind, what you can imagine happening in the future, just in what *is* this second.

P.K.: No. Nothing right this second, but—

Critter (*holding up one hand*): We'll deal with the future when we get to it, when it becomes now.

Officer: You kids hungry back there? We got some leftover pizza up here. You like pepperoni?

SEVENTY-TWO

P.K.

They hand back the box of pizza, and Critter's all like, "Thank you, sir, I love pepperoni," and they're like, "Yeah, we waited for you for a few hours, so we had it delivered. So, you kids are far from home, huh?" and Critter chats with them with his mouth full.

They don't sound like the cops on the *Juvies* show on TV. I'm still wary, but the pizza smells really good after three days of camp food, and I finally give in and take a piece.

The cop who is driving sounds like he's from Boston, and the other one sounds like he's from New York. I think, *So, you're far from home, too, huh?* But I don't say anything.

They tell us they're going to drop us off at a place in Vegas called Best Care (ha—nice code name for a juvi lockup), where they'll call our parents.

Our parents. The days in the desert were so gloriously free from parents, boarding school, the world. For a moment I have an intense desire to jump out of the car, pulling Critter with me, and escape back into the canyons.

The New York officer tells us that Best Care is a nice place. "They've got bedrooms—a boys' wing and a girls' wing—and a lounge with a TV," he says.

Yeah, but it's a lockup, I think bitterly. Any way you look at it, we've been busted. They'll hold us at juvi prison—oops, I mean "Best Care"—overnight so our parents can come get us, and by this time tomorrow I'll be on an airplane heading to a life of boredom, constriction, and attempted brainwashing at the lovely parent-selected boarding school of my worst dreams.

SEVENTY-THREE

CRITTER

So they're just cops—they're not *the* cops. No handcuffs, but they flank us as they walk us to the front doors of Best Care. It's a long, low building with a definite we're-doing-this-on-a-shoestring-budget look to it. The orange carpeting is stained, and as we walk by the TV lounge I see that the furniture appears to have been through a few teenager tantrums and/or food fights.

The officers drop us and our backpacks off with Sylvia, the thirtysomething, sweet but pragmatic intake worker.

"We'll call your parents, assign you a room, and set you up an appointment with a counselor this evening," says Sylvia.

"I need an appointment with a shower," I tell her.

She sniffs, then nods. "How about we get you to your rooms right away," she says. She runs through a list of rules, reciting them as if she has said them a thousand times: "No alcohol, no tobacco products; all perfume, cologne, nail polish, and razors need to go in these bags"—she hands us each a ziplock bag—"and I'll keep them for you."

"We don't have any of that stuff," says P.K. "We've been camping."

Sylvia gives her a blank stare, then asks us to show her the contents of our packs. We unceremoniously dump everything onto the floor at her feet. She rummages through the pile of ropes, Camalots, carabiners, slings, jar of peanut butter, etc., looking a bit baffled. Finally, she picks up the peanut butter knife and puts it into a ziplock bag. She motions for us to pack everything else up again.

Sylvia pulls out a couple of boxes from a closet. "For after your showers, there's some donated clothing in here," she says. "And some packages of new underwear and socks— hopefully you'll find something that fits." I pick out some clean clothes, and she gives me a towel.

"I'm not going *near* the showers," P.K. mutters.

"All right," Sylvia says. "Let's get your parents on the phone then, shall we?"

I would much rather fight off rapists in the shower than talk to my parents. Sylvia points me to my room.

There's a kid in my room. Actually, it turns out to be *our* room. His name is Jeremy and he's fourteen years old and looks like he weighs around two hundred pounds. He seems nice.

"Soap is in the john," Jeremy says. "And if you're under suicide watch, you're not allowed to lock the door."

"No problem," I say. "Thanks."

Hot water coming out of pipes indoors—truly one of the marvels of the modern world. I wash off days of sweat, sun-

block, chalk, and red desert dust, and wonder how P.K. is
doing talking to her parents.

SEVENTY-FOUR

P.K.

I guess I knew I couldn't go forever without talking to them.
Sylvia gives me the choice: either I make the call or she'll call
and talk first. "You first," I say.

She dials the number and I try to stay in the moment like
Critter says. *They haven't answered the phone yet. My dad's
not shouting at me yet. My mom isn't sobbing about how worried she's been and how could I put her through this . . . yet.*

"Yes, Mr. Aubrey? This is Sylvia at Best Care runaway
shelter in Las Vegas, Nevada, and we have your daughter P.K.
here. Yes, she's fine. The state police brought them in just
now. *Them*, yes, a boy is with her. No, no, he hasn't been
arrested. They're both just runaways, not criminals, Mr. Aubrey. Yes, she's right here waiting to talk to you. Absolutely,
we'll do everything we can to keep them here until you get
here. Sir, as I said before, there is nothing against the law
about being a runaway and we cannot lock them up. We give
them a safe place—yes, I'll put her on."

I wince as I put my hand out for the phone. I put the re-
ceiver to my ear. "Hi, Daddy," I say in a small voice.

In that instant—in the fraction of a beat between "Hi,

Daddy" and when he starts talking—I know that I am open. I am giving him a chance, because even through the phone line I can feel the essence of him, of the loving father who has always been a stable, reliable presence in my life. I know that if he were to open up and say, "We love you, P.K. We want you to come home. Let's talk, and Mom and I will listen to what you have to say," then I'd be on the next plane out of here and I'd throw my arms around them both and be glad to be back in my own room. . . .

But he blows it. He *so* blows it. He starts in about how immature and inconsiderate I'm being and do I have any idea what I've put Mom through and how much it cost to hire a private investigator to find me, and don't think for one minute that this is getting me out of going to boarding school, where he has already sent a huge down payment, and on and on. But I'm not really listening. I am sitting back, observing it all, pleasantly surprised to hear that Critter and I can walk out of Best Care whenever we want to, and wondering if we'll be able to find Dante back at the campground because he has my tent in his car.

I talk to Mom, who is predictably sobbing, and lie to her, promising that I'll be here tomorrow when Dad comes to pick me up. When I hang up the phone I am shaking, but at that moment Critter comes walking down the hall whistling. He's all clean and rosy, wearing his own pants and a tight button-down shirt with large black and red checks on it that he got out of the clothes box.

I smile. "Nice shirt."

"It's totally retro," he says. "I like it."

"We can use it to play checkers on if we get bored," I say.

"Now, Christopher," says Sylvia. "Let's get your parents on the phone."

"My name's not—" Critter begins.

"You call first," I tell Sylvia. Then I quickly pull Critter out of earshot. "We're not locked in here," I whisper.

"I know," he says. "I talked to this kid Jeremy. He's apparently my roommate. He says he runs away a couple times a month, does some panhandling, then either goes to the movies or buys a bunch of comic books. He's a ward of the state because his mom doesn't want him back, so he pretty much lives here, which is kind of sad, but he seems okay with it."

"All right, so we run?" I ask. "No matter what your parents say, we're out of here?" I'm afraid that Critter's mom or dad will give him that opening—the one my dad didn't give me—and he'll want to go home.

He nods. "Anytime you want."

SEVENTY-FIVE

CRITTER

When we rejoin Sylvia, who is now talking to my parents, I see that she's getting the famous Bellarico Family Champion Worriers third degree.

"Yes, Mrs. Bell—no, not a psychiatrist, she's a social—no, I'm sorry, she can't prescribe med—all right, I'll write them down, but we can't—yes, Zoloft, uh-huh, clozapine, of course, that we can do, I'll make sure someone is with—yes, he's right here."

Sylvia holds the phone out to me. She seems extremely relieved to get rid of it.

My mother's voice. I feel the neuron blasts in my head and in my heart as she talks. Confused neurons. There's the pull: Mom, who could always make everything okay when I was little, who saved my life, and whom I love from the depths of me. And there's the push: For God's sake, I'm almost a man. Would you stop worrying and leave me alone for once?

She's freaked. She's more freaked that I haven't been taking "my meds" (they are *so* not mine) than that I've hitchhiked across the country. Dad gets on the other line. They both want to know how I'm feeling, if I've been "seeing strange things" again. (My mistake—I should never have told them about seeing between the molecules to the light underneath, or seeing the part of each person's spirit that doesn't fit inside their body and shines around them as moving colors, or any of the other things I see that they don't.) "I'm fine," I keep saying. "I feel great. I'm not depressed at all, not even for a second." That seems to help, but when I tell them I'm better without the meds, they both freak again and demand to speak to Sylvia.

P.K. and I stand there as Sylvia speaks in aborted sentences and writes down the names of two antipsychotic drugs, three antidepressants, the names and numbers of two different shrinks in the Las Vegas area, and the name of the nearest hospital with a psychiatric ward. Sylvia tries to tell them that Best Care isn't responsible for getting all of the necessary medical attention for me, but they obviously don't want to hear that. In the end she promises to put me under a suicide watch and says she'll have someone take me to a psychiatrist in the morning. When she hangs up the phone she looks exhausted.

Leave it to my parents to try to have me medicated and committed without even thinking about bringing me home. I wish I could take their fear—the whole massive ball and chain of it—and blast it out of the universe.

SEVENTY-SIX

P.K.

Suicide watch. This effectively ruins all my hopes of simply walking out the back door to freedom.

Sylvia rubs her forehead like this whole thing has given her a big headache. "All the counselors are out with the kids," she says. "They took them to a movie. Christopher, I'm going to have to ask you to sit here with me until they get back, and then I'll assign a counselor to keep an eye on you for the night."

Critter gives me a sideways glance, like, *Well, this is annoying.*

"I'll stay with him." It's that kid Critter told me about—Jeremy. I didn't even notice him, but he must have been listening to everything.

Sylvia glares at Jeremy. "*You* are supposed to be working on homework. Isn't that why you stayed back from the movie?"

Jeremy snorts. "No. I stayed here because they were going to see some lame PG kid movie."

Sylvia sighs. I can see she would dearly love to be rid of us. "All right, fine, the two of you can go watch TV in the lounge. But sit where I can see you." She looks down at my paperwork. "I'll take Peeky to her room, and I'll be right back."

I won't be needing the room because we're not staying, but I let her lead me there anyway. And I let her think we are the climbing team of Christopher and Peeky.

"My" room has someone living there already. She must be out at the movie, but I smell her scented candles as I walk in. Both beds are neatly made, and one has a pink stuffed elephant along with several Beanie Babies on the pillow. One dresser is bare, the other has framed photographs arranged on it. In a cheap plastic frame is a photo of a girl, maybe twelve or thirteen years old, standing arm in arm with a woman who looks a lot like her. They are both smiling. It is summer, with green trees in the background. In another frame is the same girl with a man. He's got his arm around her, but his smile looks bored, like he wishes he were someplace else. I pick up the photos and look from one to the other. Mom, dad, divorced, splitting time with the kid. I wonder what made her run away, what has made her live here long enough to collect stuffed animals.

The idea of taking a shower in this place still gives me the creeps, but I wash my face and brush my teeth. Then I carry my pack back to the TV lounge. I figure we need to be ready to bolt at any moment.

SEVENTY-SEVEN

CRITTER

Jeremy wants to know the gory details. "How did you do it, man? I mean, did you, like, slit your wrists and not cut deep enough, or try to shoot yourself and the gun didn't go off? Or did you hang—"

"No," I say. "None of those things." Jeremy is looking at me expectantly, like I owe him the rest of the answer because he freed me from Sylvia's clutches. I see there is no getting rid of him. "I did the car-in-the-garage thing—the whole carbon monoxide extravaganza."

"Hmm," says Jeremy, nodding knowingly, quite possibly imitating his therapist. I half expect him to say, "Do you want to talk more about that? How did that make you feeeel?" But instead he shows me his arms. "I slit my wrists," he says. "But I didn't hardly cut deep enough. They said it was a cry for help and not a real suicide attempt."

Now it's my turn to nod knowingly as I admire the thin white scars on his wrists.

We are saved from this eerie exchange of how-I-tried-to-do-myself-in stories by P.K. returning from her room. She flops into a chair and drops her pack on the floor. She smells like mint toothpaste.

"So," she says quietly. "If we stay here tonight, I get picked up by my dad in the morning. He's taking the red-eye."

"And I get dragged to a shrink who's been prepped by my parents," I say. "The last time that happened, I ended up on more drugs than a baseball player."

"Ouch," says P.K.

"I've got you covered," says Jeremy.

We both look at him.

"What—?" I begin.

"Just trust me," Jeremy says. "When I say 'Go,' start walking, go out the front doors, and don't stop. And whatever you do, *don't run*."

P.K. and I look at each other and then back at him. He widens his eyes at us. "You got a better idea?" he demands, annoyed.

"No, we trust you," I say quickly. What choice do we have?

Jeremy sits back in his chair. The television drones on in the background—some drama show none of us is interested in. He fixes his eyes on me. "So, what was it like?" he asks. "Before it and after it—what was it like for you?"

I see that his plan to help us escape is being held hostage, and in order to free the hostage I will need to bare my soul. I don't mind telling him, though—he gave up on himself once, too. And I don't mind P.K. hearing. I trust her.

"Before it," I say, "absolutely sucked. It was like every cell in my body was blah and gray. Like there was nothing bright or interesting anywhere, like life was just boring and sad and meaningless. I decided I just couldn't stand being *me* any-more."

Jeremy nods, and I know he has felt the same thing.

Now during it, during the carbon-monoxide-induced-death part, that was the amazing part. But Jeremy didn't ask about that, so I decide not to rattle him with the whole tunnel-of-light thing, and seeing my grandfather, and being shown how we are spirit inhabiting this make-believe world of form so we can have this rollicking adventure, and how everything we think of as solid is actually illusion and we can mess around with it and have fun with it—really, how the whole thing can be a blast if we realize there is never anything to be afraid of, ever. I mean, what's there to be afraid of when no one ever really dies? (Grandpa showed me that—he looked terrific, and he's been "dead" for five years.) Anyway, I decide to pick up with the "after" story.

"After it was when I woke up on the sidewalk and my mom was crying and doing CPR on me. But I felt *great*—I mean, besides being sick as a dog from the carbon monoxide poisoning, and throwing up all over the grass. But instead of my cells being gray, they were, like, sparkling, and I felt happy for the first time in ages—"

"Critter!" P.K. shakes my arm suddenly, her eyes wide. "Can I talk to you a minute?" She jerks her head toward the hallway.

"Can't it wait until after the story?" Jeremy asks.

"We'll just be a second," P.K. tells him.

She drags me out of the room, closer to Sylvia's station but out of Jeremy's earshot.

"What are you doing?" she whispers frantically.

"Uh . . . telling Jeremy the story he asked to hear?" I say, as if this is a guessing game.

"You sound like an advertisement for botched suicide attempts!" she says. "That kid has already tried it once. You're older, he obviously looks up to you, and you're telling him how locking yourself in the garage with the car running solved all your problems? Are you *kidding* me?"

I'm silent a moment. "It didn't solve all my problems by a long shot," I say.

"Then make that *clear*," P.K. says, as if she'll beat me to a pulp if I don't do exactly that.

We walk back in together and sit down.

Jeremy looks at me expectantly. "Okay, so your cells went from gray to sparkling," he says.

I rub my hands together. "Well, see, the point is, our cells *are* sparkling. All the time. I just couldn't see that before, and I very nearly died in that garage, and if I had, I would have missed out on the whole rest of my life. Which would have sucked. I just got really lucky that my mom saved me."

I glance at P.K. to see how I'm doing, and she gives me a small nod.

"Anyway," I continue, "when I came to, I saw things differently. I could see how everything is made of light, of vibration, and how our senses say, 'This is a chair' and 'This is a blade of grass,' but actually, it's all just orbiting molecules that are mostly empty space. It's all just light vibrating at different frequencies, and I could see it, literally with my eyes. I started telling my parents what I saw, and they freaked. I even found books—*science* books about quantum physics and string theory, and they explained the light and the vibration, just the way I could see it. But my parents still freaked. They were scared I'd try to off myself again, and convinced I'd gone insane. They took me to a shrink and he scared them even more. He told them I was psychotic—'visual phenomena,' he said." I take a deep breath, remembering. "The three of them had me committed."

Jeremy leans forward. "And that's where they put you on the drugs?" he asks.

"Yeah, they're big into drugs on the psych ward," I say. "Don't get me wrong. There are people who need the meds, people who are way depressed and need the antidepressants, or who've got demons in their heads if they don't take their antipsychotics. That just wasn't me. I wasn't depressed anymore *at all*, and I never had scary voices in my head or anything. For me, the drugs were a waste of Blue Cross Blue Shield dollars."

"How many years ago was all this, Critter?" P.K. asks. "And how did you finally make it out of the psych ward?"

"I got out of the psych ward by escaping," I say. "And that was . . . last week."

P.K.'s mouth drops open, but there is no time to indulge her utter astonishment because at that moment it sounds as if the entire casts of *Oliver!* and *Annie* come crashing through the front doors of Best Care.

"Go," says Jeremy.

Neither P.K. nor I move.

"Go, *now*," Jeremy orders.

He is on his feet, striding toward the group of laughing,

shouting, jostling kids. P.K. and I follow. *Whatever you do, don't run.* Jeremy marches up to a kid who is—it's hard to believe—even bigger than he is. He balls up his fist and slugs the kid in the stomach. The kid whacks Jeremy upside the head, and Jeremy lets out a whining wail. "Sy-y-l-l-lvia-a-a-a!"

Sylvia leaps into the fray, along with the three adults who came in with the kids. The two boys are swinging and wrestling. As the counselors try to pry them apart, P.K. and I walk past, unnoticed, out into the night.

SEVENTY-EIGHT

P.K.

It's like there were bricks piling up, and this is the brick that topples the whole thing over. Thinks he can make clouds disappear (and seems to be able to do it). One brick. So he's weird, I can handle it. Tried to kill himself. Two bricks, but I can deal. Escaped from the loony bin just before I met him. He's certifiably nuts. Three bricks, you're out.

It's not him so much that I turn against at first. It's *me*.

I am a loser—a complete and total loser. I finally get really attracted to a guy, and he turns out to be a psycho. I am the stupidest girl on the face of the earth.

And then my anger flares and I turn against him.

We walk past the fight—and yes, I am impressed that Jeremy is getting himself pummeled and in trouble for us—past the Best Care sign with the cheery flood lamp lighting it up, and onto the city street. I turn right, toward where I can see more neon, more people and traffic. As I walk I am closing doors: to my heart, my mind, my body. Critter is walking with me, but I want him *gone*.

"Get away from me," I say. I can see it shocks him, but I don't care. "I can't believe I was so stupid—trusting you and the things you told me. Nothing to be afraid of, ever— that's *insane*! Oh right, duh, of course it's insane, because *you're* insane. You almost got me killed on that stupid climb, following your advice." I stomp my anger into the sidewalk. He is still walking behind me, not saying anything. I stop. "Look. I can take care of myself from here on out. I don't need a crazy person hanging with me, okay?" I put my hands up in a "stop, stay right there" motion and start walking backward, away from him. "This is where we split up. Go wherever you want. You can keep the sleeping bag and all that. Just leave me alone." I turn and walk quickly away.

"Where are you going?" he calls after me.

"To the campground. Dante still has my tent."

"How are you going to get there?" he asks. He starts following me again because we're getting out of earshot.

I raise up my thumb to show him, then hold it out toward the passing traffic.

SEVENTY-NINE

CRITTER

There should be a game show on television—it would be instructive—called *Which Is More Insane?* Maybe it would go over big on the Spanish channel and it would be called *¿Quién Es Mas Loco?* Contestants would have to guess which choice is the most insane.

Which is more insane? To go through life:

> A. Afraid.
> B. As an adventurer.

¿Quién es mas loco?

> A. To think constantly about the past and/or future. (Note: Past and future don't exist. They are only ideas.)
> B. To be aware of and enjoy the here-and-now. (Note: The here-and-now is the only thing that does exist.)

Which is more insane? You're a very cute teenage girl in Las Vegas late at night; should you:

> A. Hitchhike alone to a place miles outside of town, along a deserted highway?

B. Stick with the guy who cares about you?

A car slows down and stops. It's a black sedan with a wax job that reflects the streetlights like a mirror. P.K. walks toward it. Someone opens the front passenger door to let her in. I sprint. I let myself into the car's backseat before P.K. even has her door shut.

The driver looks from one of us to the other. He's middle-aged, smoking a cigarette, and wearing enough gold necklaces and rings to outfit the Rockettes. "What's this?" he says. "Bait and switch? I think I'm getting just the girl but I get both of you?"

He's blocking traffic, not moving, and horns blare as cars weave around him.

"We're not together," says P.K. "Critter, get *out.*"

A scene from *¿Quién Es Mas Loco?* comes to me. You're in a black limo-wannabe with a Las Vegas pimp. The car is not moving. Do you: A) Jump out and run like hell? B) Try to get rid of the only well-meaning person in the vehicle so you can drive off alone with the pimp?

I sit there, refusing to move. I also refuse to shut the car door, so that if Mr. Please-don't-mistake-me-for-a-nice-guy tries to drive, he's liable to get scratches on his ride.

"I don't got work for boys, only girls," he says. "I don't go for that queer stuff."

Very nice—at least he's honest. I tap P.K. on the shoulder. "Come on, Harry, we're out of here. You know as soon as you get your clothes off you'll be busted."

"Get out, both of you!" Mr. Honest-work-doesn't-interest-me shouts at us. "Don't waste my time."

P.K. opens her door and steps out of the car. I jump out and pull her off the road, onto the sidewalk, as the car screeches away.

EIGHTY

P.K.

"*Don't* touch me." I say it strong and harsh, so there's no question I mean it for now and for all future moments.

"I didn't want you to get hit," Critter says.

"I wasn't going to get hit," I snap.

I hoist my backpack onto my shoulders and start walking. I wish I could escape. I wish I could start over, start the whole trip again with Pinebox or Adam instead of with an escaped inmate from a mental hospital. I wish I could take back the kisses—the kisses that still haunt my imagination—so that I didn't have this *connection* to an insane person. I wish I wasn't in this seedy, whore-infested town. I wish—the feeling comes so strong and as such a surprise, it stops me. *I wish I could go home.* My shoulders sag. I look down at the laces on my hiking shoes and they blur. Quickly I lift my head up, blink back the tears, but it's no good. There's a low wall next to the sidewalk. I sit down on it hard, bury my face in my hands, and let the tears come.

EIGHTY-ONE

CRITTER

Now what am I supposed to do? Girls like it if you put an arm around them while they're crying, but not if they've just said, "Don't touch me." And they won't talk until they're good and ready, so asking dumb questions like "Are you crying because of the scary pimp encounter or because you hate me so much?" is not an option.

An older couple walks by, and the woman keeps glancing at P.K. like she might be about to ask her what's wrong. I decide that P.K. should at least look like she's not alone, so I pick a spot to sit on the wall that's close enough to appear as though I'm with her, but not so close that it will piss her off.

I watch the traffic. There's a steady stream of cars, SUVs, and pickup trucks in the road, stereo systems blaring, and an intermittent stream of people walking along the sidewalk. There are couples, groups of college kids, even a few families with sleepy children in tow. I watch a portly sixtysomething man walk by with two tall, sequin-dressed, totally hot blondes, one on each arm. An expensive night, for sure.

P.K. is sniffling and starts rummaging through her pockets. Of course! That's it—girls love it when you give them Kleenex while they're crying. I fish through my pockets and find the napkin I used while eating pizza in the cop car. It only has a little bit of tomato sauce on it. I hold it out to her and she snatches it. She blows her nose, then sniffs the napkin, then looks at it. "God, what is this?" she demands.

"I think it was onion-basil," I say.

She makes a face and wipes her nose with a clean part of the napkin.

She seems to be slowing down with the crying, but I still don't sense she's ready to talk. So we just sit there, silent, about two feet apart on the wall, watching the traffic and people in the city that only sleeps when it passes out.

EIGHTY-TWO

P.K.

I shiver. The crying has made me cold. My eyes feel like puffed-up slits. For some weird reason I don't want Critter to see me looking all red-nose-puffy-eyed ugly. *Why should I care?* I turn my face away from him anyway.

My brain is fuzzy, a jumble of emotions clanking around in there. I try to lay it all out, like train tracks leading to the train wreck that just happened.

Three glorious days in the canyon, in which I am smitten by the love genie, followed by several slaps upside the head in quick succession: cops, juvi overnight camp, conversation with mean Dad. Then, *bam*, I find out the person I've been trusting with my life is certifiably insane. Quicksand. That's what it feels like. Everything solid—home, possible new boyfriend, place to sleep tonight—is slipping out from under me. I glance at Critter. He's people watching like there's going to be a test on it later. He's probably afraid that if he does the wrong thing I'll freak on him again. But he's staying with me. I wonder if he had to ask himself, "What would I do if I weren't afraid?"

I close my eyes, remember the moonlit canyon. Who is Critter, really? The strong, gentle, somewhat quirky person I've been getting to know? Or just someone who belongs in an insane asylum?

The anger wells up in me again. It's not only anger at myself for being taken in by him, for believing his "no fear" philosophy and almost getting myself killed on that climb. It's anger at the disappointment. I really, really was starting to like him.

EIGHTY-THREE

CRITTER

"You know," I say. I can hardly believe I'm trying to talk to her, but the words are coming out of my mouth, so I go with it. "I got to know people on the psych ward—people with schizophrenia and other psychoses—and every single one of them had something lovable about them."

She looks at me. She's not so angry anymore. She also has no idea why I'm saying these things.

"So I'm not going to try to convince you that I'm not crazy," I say. "I'm not going to try to separate myself from my friends at the hospital."

She frowns. She's at least trying to follow my line of reasoning.

"It's like you were getting to know *me*, who I actually am," I continue. "You even knew I'd tried to kill myself and you were chill with it."

She nods.

"Now you look at me and see a label—like there's this big sign that says 'insane' and I'm behind it and all you can see is the sign."

A pained look crosses her face and I know I am right.

"It's like those kids in school who see everything according to status; everyone has a label and they won't hang out with anyone who is 'below' them."

"I'm not like that," she blurts out.

I look at her, right into her eyes. I can see the fear. I smile a little to let her know it's all okay, that I'm not angry at her for being afraid. Maybe I'd feel the same thing if I were in her position. I want her to know I understand.

EIGHTY-FOUR

P. K.

Critter is looking at me and I can see he is *not* thinking I'm just some PMS-crazed girl (which, okay, maybe I do have PMS right now) and he's not thinking how ugly I look with my nose all runny and my eyes swelled half shut. He's looking at me like . . . he accepts me. Just like that, for who I am right now. And before I know it I'm crying again, because that's what I wanted from my dad and mom on the phone and didn't get. They've got me labeled "problem teenager," "bad student," "in need of discipline," and all they can see is the labels. They can't see *me*.

Now here is someone offering me that simple acceptance. Am I going to turn him away, put him in a box marked "psych-ward escapee"? *Am* I like those superpopular girls who won't date beneath themselves? Am I so scared of the stigma of craziness, so afraid that hanging with him makes me a loser? Another label.

I blink and let the tears run down my cheeks.

"I'll try," I say. "I'll try to get beyond the labels." It's all I can promise him.

"Deal," he says.

EIGHTY-FIVE

CRITTER

Then, right away, she's all about the tent.

"So, can we please hitchhike together out to the campground now?" she pleads. "I spent three hundred and forty-seven dollars on that tent. I don't exactly want to give it to Dante."

The theme music from *¿Quién Es Mas Loco?* starts playing.

"P.K., I think we need to get out of town, as in out of the *state*, as fast as we can," I say. "Before . . . your dad gets here."

I don't tell her it's not really her dad we're running from.

It's *the* cops we're running from—the ones who are after me. I knew the cops with the pizza weren't *the* cops when they didn't handcuff me. Those must have been the cops that were on P.K.'s trail, sent by the private investigator and all that. All they knew, apparently, was that P.K. was with someone—a "friend of her cousin's"—who they assumed was a runaway, too. Just a runaway.

Images flash in my head of Maria, the day *the* cops brought her back. She'd walked out, set off the alarms, headed for the bridge. They caught her before she could jump. The commotion when they brought her in was surreal: Maria, angry and struggling, her hands cuffed behind her back, her legs in shackles; one of *the* cops shoving her when she refused to walk; Maria's mother screaming, "She's not a criminal! Why are you treating her like this?"

It's not a crime to run away from home. But to run away from a mental hospital when you have been diagnosed psychotic, and therefore "a danger to yourself and others," is another story. I guess it makes sense—the consequences are too dire when someone goes off their meds and the voices say "kill" and they do it.

I went to see Maria in her room later that night. The miracle of modern drugs had reduced her to a drooling stupor. And then they moved her to another hospital, one with bigger bolts on the doors.

I have no doubt that *the* cops, the ones who have been sent by the hospital for me, have now been clued in by my clueless parents, and are quickly closing in.

"My dad isn't getting here until morning," P.K. says. "We've got time. I want my tent!"

The theme music fades; time for the show to start:

A. Go to campground to make girl happy, giving *the* cops plenty of time to find you.

B. Keep on lying about why you need to race out of town in the hopes that girl will change her mind about $347 tent in time for you to avoid *the* cops' ambush.

C. Run off on your own and leave very cute girl to hitchhike alone to a place miles down a deserted road . . . wait, wasn't this from a previous episode?

D. Tell it like it is.

EIGHTY-SIX

P.K.

"Oh my God, Critter, aren't you *scared*?" I'm hyperventilating, and he's perfectly calm.

"Well, no, there's no cops here right this second," he says.

I throw my hands in the air. "Why didn't you tell me sooner?" I demand.

"You were . . . busy."

I suddenly feel like a total jerk, being all self-absorbed when Critter is about to be handcuffed, drugged, and locked up. "We need to get out of here *now*!" I say firmly. I see a taxicab and flag it down.

Critter doesn't object. He slides into the backseat beside me.

"Bus station, please," I tell the cab driver.

"I've got some cash left, but probably not enough for bus tickets out of town," Critter says.

"Not a problem," I say. I flash him my check card. "I figure now that my parents know where I am, I can use it."

He nods. "Get cash for the tickets though, or it'll all be traceable."

I lean forward. "I need to stop at an ATM, too," I tell the driver.

I sit back in the seat.

"So, where are we going?" Critter asks. He's smiling, and I can tell he's thinking "adventure" rather than just "escape."

I look up, purse my lips. "Hawaii?"

"You did say bus station, not airport, right?" he says.

"How about wherever the next bus is going," I say. It feels breathless, like abandon, to be so daring.

He nods approvingly.

The driver pulls over at an ATM, and I jump out of the cab to get the cash. I think of all those evenings spent babysitting the neighbor's kids, and how it is now translating into this escape/adventure.

When I return to the cab, Critter says, "I'll pay you back."

My mind shoots to the future: Critter working, waiting tables at some grungy diner in the desert somewhere, coming back to the trailer he and I are living in, counting out bills from his tips, and saying, "There you go, all paid up." For a moment I wonder, *Where are we going?* Are we leaving our families, school, our old lives, just like that? Will we stay on the run, hide out, keep under the radar *forever*?

"Oh man, what's the matter?" Critter asks.

I shake myself out of it. "Nothing," I say.

"You mean you don't want to tell me," he says flatly.

He's obviously read my mind, or at least my mood, again.

"I was in the future," I say. "I'm back in the moment now."

That shuts him up. And, truly, I do come back to the moment, and the fact that we'd be incredibly stupid to return to our families right now because of dire consequences, so being on the run is perfect. I smile at him. "Right *now*, we're on the way to the bus station," I say, "and you're about to owe me some bucks."

EIGHTY-SEVEN

CRITTER

The mustard-yellow fades and she's got her signature rosy peach creeping back in, so I believe her that she's feeling better. I wonder what she was thinking. Maybe she was worried that we're too late and there won't be any buses leaving until morning and we'll get found, asleep on the bus station floor by both her father and *the* cops.

Just past the LIVE GIRLS flashing neon sign, the cab pulls up in front of the bus depot. We pay the driver and climb out.

We walk into the small station. A television blares. People sit on chairs, on the floor, and on their luggage. There are a few sleeping babies strewn across laps. Out back three or four buses sit, idling—an excellent sign that we'll be able to leave tonight. The bus to Los Angeles is announced, and the people on the floor rise like zombies, file out, and start loading luggage into the side of one of the buses.

P.K. and I look at each other. I know she's thinking there are no rocks in L.A.

"Well, it'll get us out of here fast, anyway," she says.

"We don't have to stay in L.A.," I say. "We could go up the coast from there—how about San Francisco?"

We get in line at the ticket window.

"Aren't there like a gazillion runaways and street kids in San Francisco?" P.K. asks.

"Hippie Hill. The beat goes on," I say.

"Huh?"

"Hippie Hill. It's this place in Golden Gate Park near Haight-Ashbury. There's been a drumming and drug party going on there since the 1960s."

"Long party," P.K. says.

"So, we could go live on Hippie Hill, blend in with the other scuzzball runaways, become expert panhandlers, try our luck at drug overdosing . . . *or* we could go straight to the climbing shop and see if there's anyone heading out to Yosemite. It's only a few hours from there."

It's our turn at the ticket window.

"Two tickets to San Francisco," P.K. says.

The woman behind the counter explains that we'll have a two-hour layover in L.A. before we catch the bus to San Francisco.

"So, what caught your interest?" I ask as we move toward the exit doors. "Was it the drugs or the panhandling?" I stop at a vending machine and buy some gum.

P.K. just smiles and hands me one of the tickets.

"Last call, Los Angeles," comes the voice over the loud-speaker.

We run out the door to our escape vehicle.

EIGHTY-EIGHT

P.K.

On the bus I choose the window seat and we settle in—throw our packs on the ceiling rack, lean our seats back, ball up jackets to use as pillows.

"You comfy?" Critter asks.

"Yep," I say.

People around us are dealing with carry-on bags, getting their iPods adjusted, crinkling plastic from snacks. The bus revs into gear, backs out of the parking spot, and heads toward the highway.

Yosemite Valley. Just "the Valley" for short. The yardstick

all other climbing areas are measured by. The place so many legends got started: Royal Robbins, Yvon Chouinard, Warren Harding. Not to mention Lynn Hill doing the first free ascent of The Nose before any guy was able to do it. I wonder if we've got enough cash to buy bivy gear and do one of the multiday climbs where you sleep on the wall, suspended above the earth, far from the clutches of cops and parents.

"Camp Four," I say. Critter smiles, and I know I don't have to explain a thing. It's the place those legendary climbers lived, for months at a time, in between putting up some of the most classic climbs on the planet. I've seen pictures of it: just a simple camping area in the shadow of those towering cliffs. I'll *walk* to Camp Four from the bus station if I have to.

EIGHTY-NINE

CRITTER

The rumble of the bus engine fills my ears. P.K. looks out the window, light and shadow playing on her face.

Right now, she is with me. I have opened my heart, and she has understood. And we've got a long bus ride ahead of us to be together. We are like space travelers, winging our way to unknown worlds, pretending we are not caught in the orbit of a dark planet.

You will lose her, says the hamster.

I know, I say.

It's best not to argue with the hamster, especially when he

is merely stating the obvious. Arguing, resisting, only starts up the wheel. If you simply say, "I know," most of the time he'll just shrug and creep away.

NINETY

P.K.

Critter seems . . . sad. What's up with that? Scared of the people who want to lock him up, worried that they'll track us down, angry that his parents don't support him—any of that I'd understand. But *sad*? It makes no sense.

NINETY-ONE

CRITTER

A short lapse into thinking of the future, and there you have it: suffering. I snap back into the present moment, in which the girl is *here*. She's punching her jacket as if that could make it more comfortable, getting herself settled in her seat, and now she's . . . looking at me funny.

"We need scissors," she says.

"Scissors?"

"Yeah, and coloring—"

"That's it!" I slap the armrest. "We need scissors, coloring books, crayons, construction paper, paste. We won't be bored for a minute on this long bus ride. I'll buy them on our first layover stop. And don't forget, we've got my shirt, too. Checkers."

P.K. is shaking her head, looking entertained. "I was about to say we need scissors and coloring stuff for our hair. They're looking for a girl with short brown dreads, and a guy with a long blond ponytail. We can fix that."

I pull my hair to where I can see it. "I could go green, or maybe electric blue," I say.

She appraises my hair. "Probably something boring like brown or black would be better—less of an attention getter."

I try to imagine her with her dreads shorn off. Her hair is going to be way short. And she'll still be way cute.

"I think I'll go for white-blond," she says.

I nod. Definitely way cute. I give her a pleading look. "Can we still get the coloring books and crayons?"

"Critter, we're going to *sleep* on this bus ride. Aren't you tired?"

NINETY-TWO

P.K.

Critter opens his pack of gum and gives me some. Cinnamon.

"This is one time it'll be okay to fall asleep with gum in our mouths," I say.

"Why?" he asks, folding several pieces into his mouth.

"Because if we wake up with it in our hair, we were going to cut it off anyway." I reach out to touch the end of his ponytail. It's baby soft. I wonder if he feels like it's part of him like my dreads are part of me. I think of all those runaway-slave stories I've read, where the person has to risk losing everything—their loved ones, their limbs, even their lives, for one chance at freedom. Hair just isn't that big a deal.

"My ponytail was my best smuggling device at the hospital," he says. "Like that hundred-dollar bill from my sister? No way they would have let me keep it. They go though your stuff all the time. So I kept it rolled up tiny, hidden in my hair, under the rubber band."

"How did you wash your hair?" I ask.

He shrugs. "I just never took the rubber band out. The bill got a little soggy, that's all."

I suppress a grin. "I hope you won't miss it too much—the ponytail, I mean."

"Nah," he says. "I've got pockets." He leans his head back against the seat.

The motion of the bus is making me sleepy. I spit my gum out—I don't really want to wake up with it in my hair—and once again try to make my jacket into a comfortable pillow. I yawn. "Good night, Critter," I say.

"Night," he says. He is almost instantly asleep, his breathing deep and rhythmic. I close my eyes, let my body move with the jostling of the bus, and wait for sleep to take me over.

What are you doing? It's my own thoughts, interrupting my voyage into dreamland. *I mean, what the hell do you think you're doing? Maybe you're the crazy one. How long do you think you can fend them off? The only way he'll be free is if he stays on the run. What do you think you're buying with these haircuts? Two weeks of climbing at Yosemite before you get caught? Six hours if they find you fast? A lifetime of freedom? Do you really want to stay on the run with this guy for years? You don't owe that to him. All you need is a couple more weeks to climb in the Valley, get some good routes in, feel free for a while longer. Then you can let your folks catch up to you, and by then they'll probably be ready to skip the whole boarding school thing. You won't get homeschooling, but you can promise to do better in school next year, yada yada, and then you'll take summer classes—yuck—to make up for missing the end of the semester, and voilà, you've got your old life back. Not perfect, but a whole lot better than either boarding school or giving up your entire life as you know it. So, you're going to get caught soon—very soon. And he is going to be locked up. Handcuffed, drugged, and locked up. And there's nothing you can do about it.*

I'm wide awake now, watching the lights shift across the ceiling with each passing car. The guy in the seat next to us is snoring. The lady in front of us has her iPod on loud enough that I can hear the tinny music throbbing.

Is there something I can do about it—about Critter? Short of staying on the run with him, using my bank card at ATMs, being the one who figures out how to evade "*the* cops," as he calls them? But what kind of life would that be? I'd never finish high school, never get to college, never see my family again. . . .

Critter shifts and opens his eyes sleepily. "Shhhh," he says.

"What do you mean, 'shhhh'? I didn't say anything," I say, annoyed.

He shakes his head. "It was the wheel, squeaking," he says.

I think he must be dreaming, talking in his sleep. But then he says, "Stop arguing with the hamster or he'll keep you running on the wheel all night long."

I scowl at him in the darkness. How did he *know*? He closes his eyes and goes back to sleep. I punch my jacket-pillow angrily and try to get comfortable. He read my mind while he was asleep; how annoying is that? Maybe the boy *should* be locked up. I close my eyes, determined not to let my thoughts start another interminable argument. I rest my awareness on the present moment: rumble of bus engine, smell of peanut butter crackers someone is eating, my own breathing, scratchy bus seat against my skin, no cops here right now. . . . I drift off to sleep.

NINETY-THREE

CRITTER

Sunrise in the smog over the freeway, a couple of hours outside Los Angeles: just as much perfection and possibility as any other day.

P.K. is still asleep as the bus pulls into another town, another bus depot. The bus driver says we have a fifteen-minute layover. Anyone interested in breakfast can run in and buy something.

I go into the dingy bus station and buy a California map and two bagels with cream cheese. When I return, P.K. is awake. She stretches and yawns, covering her mouth. "I want my toothbrush," she says.

When she returns from the luxurious bus bathroom, I've got the map open. I hand her a bagel.

"Hey, doesn't the bus go up through Fresno on the way to San Francisco?" I ask.

"Yep," she says, her mouth full of bagel.

"It looks like we should get out there," I say. "It looks like it's even closer to Yosemite than San Francisco."

She examines the map and agrees with me. Then she says, "I want to know something." She's got that the-next-question-you-hear-is-going-to-nail-you look in her eyes. I brace myself. "How do you always know what I'm thinking?"

There it is. I'm nailed. Unless I can squirm away. I shrug. "Just some lucky guesses." I can't tell her about the colors. That was the last straw for Mom and Dad—the thing that made them decide to commit me. "Psychotic visual phenomena," the shrink called it. I guess that was on top of the fact that Grandpa visited me a couple more times with messages for Mom and Dad, which added "auditory hallucinations" to my list of symptoms.

P.K. looks at me hard. "There's something you're not telling me," she says. "I can see it in your eyes."

Just what I needed to wriggle free. "So, you could see it

in my eyes. Don't you think maybe I just see things in your eyes, too?"

"Critter, last night you had your eyes *closed*, and it was dark, plus I was turned away from you, looking out the window, and you *still* knew what I was thinking. How do you *do* that?"

She's getting upset. I remember last night. The colors were vivid, black and slate-gray boiling so violently it woke me up. How can I explain that? I'm hooked into her, that's all. "Last night I didn't know *what* you were thinking," I say quietly. "I just knew you had thoughts going around and around in circles and that they weren't good, and they weren't going to let you sleep unless you stepped out of them because that's what thoughts like that always do. That kind of thinking never gets you anywhere."

"But *how*?" She plops her half-eaten bagel down on her lap. "How did you know? Are you psychic? Are you telepathic? Do you have ESP? Is your mother named Madame Rosetta and you grew up learning how to read tea leaves and see things in a crystal ball? *What?*"

"Actually, my mom is named Charlotte and she's a pediatric nurse and she's about the most practical, down-to-earth person you'll ever meet," I say.

P.K. cocks her head. "So she's not peace-and-love earthy-crunchy anymore?" she asks.

"She's still earthy-crunchy," I say. "She works at an inner-city clinic and is into the whole social justice thing."

P.K. folds her arms over her chest and huffs. "Now you're trying to distract me, talking about your mom. I want to know how you always know what I'm thinking."

The real answers race through my mind: I see *you*—the part of your spirit self that doesn't fit into your body, and floats around it—in colors and movement. When I died, it stripped away the veils. I can see through the stuff we call "matter" and it isn't solid at all. It's swirling energy. Our thoughts are the same kind of energy, just swirling at a higher frequency. Science is discovering it, but I can see it and feel it. Scientists are guessing at it, but I *know* it.

What good would it do if I told her? Give her mind another reason to see me as a nutcase? Confuse her? Scare her? As the real answers press in on me, I give her another fake answer.

"I don't know," I say.

She's pissed. She turns away from me, toward the window, and eats the rest of her bagel in silence.

NINETY-FOUR

P.K.

I am way too tired for this bull. I guess if he doesn't want to tell me, I can't force him. I finish eating, mumble, "Thanks for breakfast," and curl up to go back to sleep. We're on the freeway now, heading toward L.A. I might as well sleep until we have to transfer to the northbound bus.

NINETY-FIVE

CRITTER

Maybe it's because she lets go, doesn't keep pressing the issue. Maybe it's because I wriggled free successfully, so now I can make my own choice about it. Or maybe it's just that her silent treatment is working. Anyway, I say, "I see colors."

She opens her eyes. "What?"

"I see colors. That's how I know what you're feeling and thinking. I see colors around you—they move and they change."

She nods, closes her eyes. "What am I thinking now?" she asks.

Calm, slow-moving peach-colored light surrounds her. "Something good and peaceful," I say.

She smiles. "Very good. I was thinking about sleep." She looks out the window, frowns a bit. I don't even need to see the mustard-yellow seep into her colors to know she has started worrying about something. "What am I thinking now?" she asks.

"It's on your face and in your colors, and it's not good," I say.

"I was hating all this L.A. smog," she says. "It's already thick as soup and we're still an hour away. So, you don't know *what* I'm thinking, just the mood of it?"

"Right," I say.

She looks right at me. "Thanks for telling me, Critter," she says. And she curls back up to go to sleep.

NINETY-SIX

P. K.

Colors, huh? I don't doubt him. I just never would have guessed it.

I fall asleep watching the patterns of colors that float behind my eyelids. I wonder if that's what it's like for Critter. I dream of color—hair color. We're in Yosemite and Critter is sitting on top of a high cliff. His hair is loose and flowing and it's indigo-blue, the color of the desert sky. For some weird reason I've got one of those old-fashioned round mirrors in my hand. I look at myself. My dreads stick out around my head like a halo—a halo the color of a ripe peach. Even in the dream it makes me laugh. What a ridiculous color for hair.

The screech of bus brakes and the voice over the bus's speaker system wake me. Los Angeles. We've got enough layover time to get to a drugstore.

NINETY-SEVEN

CRITTER

She is suddenly all about the hair.

"Come on, we've got to buy hair dye," she says. We leave the bus station, walk past a McDonald's and down a street lined with old low factories with lots of broken windows. It doesn't necessarily look like the kind of neighborhood where you'd find a Walgreens, but there are other people walking on the sidewalks, so maybe they know something I don't. We come to a corner and have to wade through a mean-looking bunch of guys in baggy pants and sunglasses. They stare at us. Suburban kids with backpacks are probably not the norm around here. P.K. has no idea where she is—she's just mono-focused on hair dye.

"P.K., I think we should go back to the bus station. We can get the stuff in Fresno—" I begin. But she shakes my hand off her arm and marches ahead of me. I hear a snicker from one of the mean-guy watchers. They're following us. Are they about to get into our business?

"What you got in that pack?" One of the thugs—a kid, really, maybe close to our age—shouts at us. His words are laced with a Spanish accent. I think we might be on some-one's turf.

"P.K.!" I say it sharp and quick. She turns around. I mo-tion, *Let's go back.*

"I said, what you got in that pack?" The kid steps in front of me. He's stocky, muscular. His hand goes to his jacket pocket. Time to come clean about what's in the pack.

"Climbing gear," I say.

Out of my peripheral vision I see the others coming, saun-tering. I'm being surrounded by Spanish-speaking hoodlums in designer sunglasses.

I consider my choices:

1. Tell P.K. to run and let the burrito brothers beat the stuffing out of me.

2. Bust out with lightning-fast karate moves, take the whole group of them down, then walk away with P.K. on my arm.

3. Dump out the contents of my pack and spend a pleasant half hour explaining to the enraptured group how each type of climbing gear is used.

4. Stand here, unmoving, and wait for something to happen.

I choose number four.

"Anybody know where we can get some hair dye?" P.K.'s voice cuts through the tension.

I want to say, *Uh, P.K., we're about to become gang fodder, would you please give up on the hair dye?* But when I glance at her, she is clearly terrified. I am relieved. At least she gets it.

"Hair dye?" The stocky kid, obviously the leader, says slowly.

"Yeah," I say, running with the ball P.K. has thrown. "We came from Nevada and we're on the bus to Fresno. We're being chased by the cops, and we need to change our hair color so they won't catch us." There you go: we're not from your town, we're on our way out just as fast as you want us out. And we're being chased by the law. That's got to score points around here.

"My aunt's store is near here. She sells hair stuff," one of the guys says.

The group begins to move, and I realize we're getting an

escort to Auntie's store. Nobody talks. They just walk in an amoeba shape, with us in the middle, to a small, beat-looking corner store. The leader guy motions for us to go in. They stay outside while P.K. looks through the boxes of hair stuff and I stand behind her. Neither of us says a word. Her hands are shaking.

At the cash register, a young woman with round dark eyes rings us up. She keeps glancing out the door at the guys standing there. As we go to leave, she comes with us.

If I'd taken Spanish in school instead of German, I would understand the words of what happens next. Instead, I see the whole thing in a Technicolor of emotions. Auntie is bright-red angry, fed up, asking questions, giving orders. The tough-as-iron, bite-me street kids are chastised (muted orange), trying to stay steely, but also wanting to show respect to Auntie. When it's all over, Auntie turns to me and P.K. "They will walk you to the bus station," she says.

And they do.

NINETY-EIGHT

P.K.

Oh my God.

When we get to within grenade-throwing distance of the bus station, the Crips or Bloods or whatever they are stop walking and stand there watching us go. I'm still shaking inside, but Critter is calm and collected. I half expect him to turn around, wave, and call out, "Thanks, guys. See you around." But he doesn't.

Inside the bus station my heart rate finally begins to slow down, but there's some kind of energy that needs to be released. I release it on Critter. I grab his arm and spin him toward me. "How can you be so damn *calm*?" I shout at him.

He looks dumbfounded. I decide to explain. "We could have been *killed* out there. They had knives and guns—I saw them!" People are starting to stare. I lower my voice. "And you—you're not even scared. You're like . . . it didn't even happen."

Critter looks pained for a second. As if he can't begin to fathom how to explain to me what he wants to say next. Like I'm too stupid to get it. I save him the trouble. "Oh, I know," I say in a venomous whisper. "Nothing did happen, right? In the present moment I'm in a bus station"—I twirl around, my arms out for emphasis—"and I'm safe, and there are no gang members here now, right?"

He nods slowly, still looking confused by my fury. His confusion makes me even more angry. I grab his arms and shake him hard. "God, Critter, don't you even get danger? Are you, like, floating on top of the physical world as if it can't affect you?"

Even with my voice lowered, we're causing a scene. Critter takes my elbow and leads me over to some seats. He leans close to me. "You're still scared," he says quietly. "Try to let it go, P.K."

I'm seething. Frankly, I'm confused by my own feelings. Has my fear morphed into anger?

"Yes, you're safe now in a bus station," Critter says. "But you were always safe, even out there on the street."

Now I'm confused by him as well. He sees it in my eyes, or maybe in my colors.

"We just are. Safe." He shakes his head slightly, as if there is too much behind his words, too much to explain if I don't just *get* it. The problem is, I don't get it. But I feel calmer now, as if the peace in his words has reached me somehow.

Our bus, the bus to San Francisco, is announced.

"But the world can hurt me . . . can't it?" I ask.

He reaches up, puts two fingers on my forehead. I close my eyes. "Not *you*," he says. "Who *you are* is safe." He takes his fingers away and I open my eyes. "Plus," he says brightly, "it has already happened, so it follows the Law of Inevitability."

I groan and hoist my pack. "Come on," I say. "We've got a bus to catch."

We shuffle toward the loading zone. Soon we'll be in Fresno, far from the mean city, far from my dad and his plans. And soon after that, we'll be in Yosemite, with its massive granite spires.

The longing comes up in me, strong, for the rock. I need the rock now, more than ever, to push my body to the limit, to clear my mind, to bring me into the world of primal fear and wash away all these spinning fears, imagined or real, of what people may or may not do to me. The rock is simple: gravity versus me. I long for that simplicity now.

NINETY-NINE

CRITTER

We file onto the bus and everyone starts the nesting process: arranging luggage, taking off shoes, etc. One last nest before we get released into the wild.

P.K. picks the window seat again. "So really, other than for its smuggling capabilities, are you going to be sorry to lose your hair?" she asks.

"Am I going bald?" I ask.

She rolls her eyes. "You know, when I make you cut it all off. Do you feel like your ponytail is part of you?"

I shrug. "Nah. Hair is just one of those things we sort of hang on ourselves. It's like we've got this . . . I don't know, *me*-suit."

She gives me a sideways look. "Explain?"

I think a moment. "It's like this big heavy thing that drapes over our shoulders and it's got all these hooks on it, and we hang stuff on the hooks: hair, clothes, social group, things we're good at. Some people hang all this great stuff on themselves: gymnastics team, valedictorian, going to Harvard next year. Some people hang bad stuff all over themselves: fat, mean parents, depression.

"Then there's the group me-suits, where everybody has to hang the same stuff on themselves so they belong. It's not who you are, but people get so attached to all the *stuff*, they think it's who they are.

"Like my dad—he used to be this great athlete, triathlon champion, almost made the cut for the Olympics, won a few state championships. Now he's getting older, he's had a few injuries, so it's like the 'champion' badge he had hung on himself keeps falling off. He keeps trying to pick it up and hang it back up there—he works out like crazy, rehabs the last injury, tries to get his stamina back, get stronger—but it never quite works. He's not twenty-two anymore. All he does is hurt himself and feel disappointed and angry. He'll never get it back. I wish he could realize that it doesn't matter—it's just a thing he had hanging on himself. It has nothing to do with who he is."

"That's so sad," P.K. says. "Of course it has to do with who he is. Like my climbing is who I am."

She's not getting it. I try to explain again. "People think it has to do with who they are, but that's the lie. And the whole world is set up to make you believe that if you could just hang the right stuff on your me-suit, your life would be perfect finally. Like counselors who try to help kids hang different stuff on the suit: improve their grades, solve their family problems, get better friends. Or the advertising industry: use this shampoo, have this plastic surgery, lose the weight, get the body you've always wanted. The point is, *you* are not your fat, ugly, stringy-haired body. You're not your body at all."

She looks at me like I've just insulted her. I backpedal quickly.

"Let's take you, P.K., for example, okay? You've got: Five-eleven climber, trad leader, athlete-girl clothes, funky rad hair, intriguing name, unsympathetic parents, super-smart, lousy grades, way cute, don't-mess-with-me attitude, miss my brothers, middle-of-the-pack social status."

She laughs. "I guess that's sort of me in a nutshell."

"No!" I nearly shout it. "That's not you at all. That's the stuff hanging on your me-suit."

"But who am I without all that stuff?" she asks, bewildered.

"Yes! That's it. That's exactly the point," I say. *"Who are you without all that stuff?"*

ONE HUNDRED

P.K.

I don't know why, but when Critter asks me the question, *Who are you without all that stuff?* I close my eyes. Immediately I'm spinning, and I'm expanding, until it feels like I'm as big as the bus, then as big as the earth, then I expand out into the universe and I have no limits, no outline, I just *am*. I feel like I'm flying, soaring through space, and a small part of me is smiling, thinking, "Critter said I was way cute." Suddenly I jerk awake.

"Whoa," I say. "I just had this really weird dream." And then I'm embarrassed because I fell asleep in the middle of a conversation.

"That wasn't a dream," he says.

"Now you know when I'm awake and when I'm asleep?" I snap. "I just woke up, okay? I had this weird *dream*."

He shakes his head and looks a little sad, like he wishes I would believe him. But I was asleep. I know it.

"Your colors, P.K.," he says. "They went totally glitter-gold. When someone goes to sleep, their colors just go pastel."

I nod slowly. That's what it felt like. Totally glitter-gold. "I was . . . *big*. Like so much more than this little body here in this bus seat. It was like . . ." I look out the bus window, try to feel it again. "It's like there's something calm and . . . *grand* looking out at the world through my eyes."

When I look back at Critter he's got this big smile on his face. "Yeah, baby," he says. "And no NDE necessary."

I shake my head slightly. "NDE?"

"You know, the whole near-death thing I went through," he says.

Whatever. The boy makes no sense sometimes. "Can I go to sleep for real now?" I ask. "I want to try for one more nap before we get to Fresno."

He nods and puts his head back against his seat, still smiling.

ONE HUNDRED ONE

CRITTER

I *do* love it when the girl gets it. I glance over at her, curled up against the window. I wish I could grab her and kiss her, but I won't. I can't expect this realization to be permanent. She'll go back to identifying with her "image," and she'd never be able to handle the thought of "boyfriend who escaped from a mental ward" hanging on her me-suit for all the world to see. But that would never happen anyway. By the time she gets back anywhere near the people she knows, I'll be safely tucked away where I can't be a "danger to myself or others."

ONE HUNDRED TWO

P.K.

Fresno is sunny and warm with birds singing in the palm trees that line the streets. I start to wonder if we actually have to do all this crazy disguising. Can't we just go climb and have a blast?

We decide to walk to the climbing shop, which we look up in the phone book and figure is only a couple miles away. There's sure to be someone at the shop who is on their way out to Yosemite, and we'll hitch a ride.

I take a deep breath of the warm, sunlit air. "So, you really think I need to lose my dreads?"

Critter tugs at my hair playfully. "They're not coming off easy."

"Really." I try to get him to be serious. "Do you honestly think we're being tracked? I mean, there are a lot of climbing areas in this country. My dad can't possibly check up on every single one of them."

Critter shrugs. "You were the one with the 'Lady Clairol meets James Bond' escape plan. I'll do whatever you want."

"I want to keep my hair and go climb something heinous," I say.

"Let's do it," he says.

As we walk down the city street, past taquerias and dry-cleaning shops, I feel all the joy of springtime and freedom and, I have to admit it, I'm happy to be with Critter. I'm happy to be on this adventure with him, to be heading back to the rocks—and I mean *the* rocks, the Valley itself. I smile up at him. I'm really sorry we've been through so much the past couple of days and I've been so mean to him. I wish it were still just simple the way it was in the canyon at Red Rocks. If it were still that simple, I'd stop right here on the street and kiss him. But it's not.

We reach the climbing shop finally, and march up the steps to the front doors. I glance inside through the glass, and something catches my eye. Something registers on my brain as "familiar," but I don't know what it is. All I know is, it scares me, and I don't open the doors. I cup my hands around my face so I can get a better look. That's when I see it clearly. I catch my breath, move away quickly, grab Critter, and pull him down the steps with me.

"We're out of here!" I say, and take off running.

ONE HUNDRED THREE

CRITTER

Whatever she saw in there scared the daylights out of her. We run, packs bouncing on our backs, hiking shoes slapping on the sidewalk. Was her *father* in there? How could he have tracked us so fast? Cops? No way anyone could have read our minds and figured out where we were going.

P.K. drags me into a gas station mini-mart. Maybe she got the munchies and that's why we just ran here?

She pulls me toward the unisex bathroom. Aha—she had to pee really bad all of a sudden. She pushes me inside. "Stay in there, lock the door. I'll knock in a few minutes. Don't let anyone else in but me."

I stand in the grungy bathroom, breathing in the smell of camphor and old urine, trying *not* to figure out what in the world she is up to.

A few minutes later there is a knock and P.K.'s voice. "Critter, it's me. Open up."

She slips in, dumps a handful of stuff she just bought into the sink: cheese crackers, shampoo, a razor. "Lock the door," she commands. Then she picks up the package with the razor in it and starts to open it. "We'll have to get the blade out of this thing," she says.

I grab her by the shoulders, look into her eyes. "P.K., whatever you saw back there, it is not worth slitting our wrists over!"

ONE HUNDRED FOUR

P.K.

He is so earnest, so worried, I don't have the heart to laugh. I do grin, though, because his caring makes me feel really good. I slow down, too. Time to explain.

"I couldn't find scissors. The razor blade is for cutting our hair," I say. "They've got a flyer—an actual *flyer*, overnight, in color, at the climbing shop. It was hanging behind the cash register so everyone working there could see it. All I saw was your face and my face. I didn't bother to read it. Probably says, 'having too much fun, must be returned to captivity.'"

"By now, your parents and my parents and the hospital authorities have joined forces," Critter says. "So . . . I guess we'll be staying away from climbing shops for a while."

I use a thick wad of paper towels to protect my fingers and break the razor blade free. I hand it to him carefully. "Do the deed," I say.

Critter starts sawing. It hurts because it pulls, and I keep telling myself hair is not a big deal. I watch as he drops each of my dreads into the trash can.

"Done," he says finally.

"Could you even it up a little, so I don't look like a three-year-old cut it?" I ask.

He does some more sawing. "There. Now it looks like a five-year-old cut it."

I turn to the mirror, almost afraid to look. My eyes are huge. My head looks small. But I'm still myself. Time for the bleach. First, though, I tell Critter to give me the razor blade and turn around.

"What if I'm like Samson?" he asks as I cut away at his ponytail. "And all my strength was in my hair? Maybe I'll be a five-four climber now."

"Here." I hand him the ponytail, intact in its red rubber

band. "Put this in your pocket and you'll still be cranking five-twelve."

He just laughs and tosses it into the trash can on top of my dreads. I start the process of trying to give him a classic short haircut.

"Ow," he says. "How much of this do you have to do? I think that thing is getting dull."

"Stop your whining," I say. "I'm trying to make you look like one of those Future Lawyers of America guys."

When I'm done, he looks more like a lightning-strike victim, but it has to be good enough. There's someone knocking on the bathroom door.

"Go away," I say loudly. "I'm going to be in here for a while."

We hear grumbling, but apparently the person leaves. I open my pack and pull out the hair color we risked our lives for in L.A. "Here, read directions." I shove the "Chestnut" box at Critter and tear open the "White Golden Blond" box.

I lean my head over the sink, do a fast shampoo job, then mix and shake the foul-smelling stuff and squirt it over my head. I spread a bit on my eyebrows, too. "This is my best imitation of a vanilla snow cone," I say.

I put Critter through the same process, and then we stand there looking at each other with goop on our heads.

"We need new names, too," I say.

"Good idea," says Critter. "Complete the new-me-suit process."

I think back to our discussion about the me-suit, and what happened when I asked myself, *What am I without all that stuff?* The expansion, the feeling like I was bigger than the bus, until I had no boundaries. Expanded Brain. "I could be E.B. instead of P.K.," I suggest.

Critter shakes his head. "Too similar."

I try again. I remember how it felt to have no boundaries. Like I was no longer any*thing*, I just *was*. Like I was just the *am* part of *I am.* Am. Amy. "Amy," I say.

"Good," says Critter. "Hi, Amy."

I smile. "Now you."

He looks up at the ceiling as if an answer is printed there. "Instead of just generic Critter, I could be a particular critter. How about Wolf or Jaguar or . . . Stallion."

I raise one foamy eyebrow at him. "You actually want me to go around calling you *Stallion*?"

He shakes his head. "You're right. Bad idea." Then his eyes brighten. "I'll be the one who kills the critters. Hunter."

"Isn't that kind of self-annihilating?" I ask.

"No. Just me-suit annihilating."

I nod. "Hello, Hunter." I reach out my hand to shake his.

"And now my scalp is burning off," he says. "Can we get rid of this stuff yet?"

My scalp and eyebrows are on fire, too, but I figure the longer I leave mine on, the blonder my hair will be, so I rinse him first. There is another knock on the bathroom door. In between making vomiting noises, I shout, "I'm sick in here! Go away."

"Very convincing," Critter says.

"Thank you," I say.

Finally I rinse off the burning glop. A little blotting

with paper towels, and we're ready to face the world: white-blond Amy with the strangely rad chop-style cut, and tall, dark, handsome Hunter, who can't afford a good hairstylist.

ONE HUNDRED FIVE

CRITTER

The guy behind the cash register hardly looks at us as we leave. I guess he didn't consider it his problem that the bathroom was tied up for almost an hour.

P.K. sees a rack of free tourist brochures and picks one up. Outside she stops to look at it. "There was a *bus*?" she blurts out.

"Huh?" I ask intelligently.

"There's a stupid *bus* that goes right into Yosemite. A bus that leaves from Merced. Do you know where Merced is?" she asks angrily. Obviously, she already knows the answer, and it is not good.

I shake my head.

"It's two stops beyond this one on the Greyhound bus line. We got off two stops early. We could have skipped the climbing shop, skipped the scary flyer sighting, skipped the whole thing, and taken buses all the way to Camp Four." She slaps the offending brochure against her thigh.

"What's stopping us now?" I ask.

"What, pay again for a bus ticket we already had?"

"Uh . . . do we have a better plan?"

She stares at me for one beat. Then we start the inevitable march back to the bus station.

The trip to Merced is about an hour. I figure before P.K. officially becomes Amy, I'd like to know how she got the name P.K. So I ask.

"It's from my great-grandmother," she says. "It was her nickname, too, and somehow I got to be P.K. Junior. She was already really old when I was a baby, but they say I used to run around yelling, 'P.K., P.K., P.K.!' whenever she came over. She died when I was three."

"So it was her nickname, too. Was *she* a preacher's kid?" I ask.

P.K. makes an annoyed face. "Why is everyone always so stuck on this preacher's-kid thing? No, she got it because of the chewing gum."

There is silence as I absorb this information. I listen to the rumble of the bus, watch lonely gas stations and highway signs go by outside the window. And absolutely nothing dawns on me about the gum. "What about the gum?" I ask finally.

P.K. is looking out the window as well. "Just one more bus ride," she says. "We're almost there."

I nod, and allow a few moments for us to feel the awe of how close we are to Yosemite. Then I start in again. "The gum?"

"Oh, you know. Wrigley's P.K. gum."

I raise my eyebrows, inviting more.

She sighs as if she has told the story too many times. "My

great-grandmother's father was a doctor, back in the days when doctors still did house calls. He used to go out in the evenings to visit sick people, and she would cry because she didn't want him to leave. She was about four years old. So he started coming home with Wrigley's P.K. chewing gum in his pocket as a treat. If she didn't cry when he left, she'd get the gum. So when he'd come to the door, she'd dance around singing, 'P.K., P.K., P.K.!' because she was all excited about her treat."

"Cool story," I say. "So it has absolutely nothing to do with her actual name or your actual name."

"Right," she says.

"So what is your actual name?" I ask.

She gives me a mischievous look. "I can't tell you that. My family is descended from leprechauns, and if you knew my real name you'd be able to control me."

"Is it Mabel?" I ask. She shakes her head. "Fioretta?" Another shake. "Gertrude?"

"That's it." She holds up one hand. "Three guesses and you're done."

"Drat," I say. "I missed my chance for a lifetime of magical wishes."

She gives me a look that I can't quite decipher. If I had to guess, though, it seems as if maybe she's starting to like me again.

P.K.

In Merced we catch the last bus of the day going to the Valley. It's filled with tourists, middle-aged couples from Iowa snapping pictures through the smudgy windows. At first Critter and I don't talk much. We just watch impatiently as the landscape goes by, flat fields of strawberries and peach trees with PICK YOUR OWN signs. Then Critter decides we need new identities.

"If people ask, we need new stories," he says. "Like whole new me-suits to go with our new hair and names."

I think a moment. "I'm a talented artist," I say. "I make this amazing jewelry from found objects, like the little flip tops from soda cans."

"But you're not wearing any jewelry," Critter says.

"Oh, that's easy to explain. If I wear anything I've made, I get these huge crowds of people gathering around me, wanting to buy it right off me. It's too much bother when I'm climbing."

Critter sits back in his seat and looks up at the ceiling in thinking mode. "And I'm a member of that—what was that club?"

"Future Lawyers of America?" I say.

"Right. I'm a member, and I have secretly applied to Harvard Law School and been accepted."

"Why did it have to be secret?" I ask.

"Because my parents are extremely rich and they would much rather I simply live on my inheritance and spend my time partying instead of wasting time studying law."

I cross my arms over my chest. "Okay, fine, so my story wasn't believable either. But do you think we really need to create these whole new lives? Can't we just climb?"

The bus is going steeply uphill now, through a forest of huge pine trees. We've finally gotten to the mountains. Critter and I are silent, watching out the window. Both of us are waiting for the big rocks to appear. There are cliffs, low ones, and a rushing river tumbling by on the right, crashing over boulders, its water frothy ice-green.

Suddenly we round a corner, and there it is: El Capitan. It rises from the valley floor, a massive block of gray granite, majestic and surreal.

"Wow!" I say softly. Critter leans over me and we press our faces to the window. It's as if there's a strong magnet in the rocks. It's pulling both of us, making our fingers and toes itch to be scaling its flanks. I feel the silence start to enter my brain—the silence that only the rocks can bring, the silence that gives me peace.

"Almost there," Critter says, and I know he feels it, too—the magnet, the silence, and the peace.

ONE HUNDRED SEVEN

CRITTER

"Are you kids really going to climb those rocks?"

I have just asked the bus driver if he'll be going near

Camp Four, the climbers' camping area, and this has alerted our fellow passengers.

"Yes, ma'am," I say as I head back to my seat. "We're hoping to."

A chorus of "Oh, my!" goes up from the flatlanders. I take a bit of pleasure in being able to impress the heck out of a group of overweight retirees from the Midwest.

"Says he'll take us right to it," I say as I flop down next to P.K./Amy.

The sun is low now. There won't be time for a route today. But just being this close to all that granite is a buzz. And there's Midnight Lightning, a classic boulder problem, right there in Camp Four. I wouldn't mind a little bouldering by moonlight.

ONE HUNDRED EIGHT

P.K./AMY

Since we have no tent, there's no camp to set up. We get dinner at the park concession: cheeseburgers and salads eaten outside at picnic tables in the waning light.

Camp Four is not nearly as rustic, grungy, or romantic as I had imagined. It's got clean, well-lighted bathrooms, and even an indoor dish-washing sink. It doesn't look like there are specific campsites, just row after row of tents, picnic tables, and bear boxes. It must be a lot bigger than when Yvon Chouinard used to stay here. One interesting thing is that

I overhear several conversations, and not one of them is in English. Climbers from all over the world are here.

No one talks to us. There is definitely a cold, aloof feeling. I guess it's the pressure to be good enough or hooked-up enough to deserve to be in Camp Four among the ghosts of the legends. It makes me glad I'm Amy and not P.K.

We head straight for Midnight Lightning, where three guys are sharing a crash pad and working out the moves.

"Hey," Critter says.

"Umph," one of the guys says as he falls and hits the crash pad.

The next guy goes up, falls at the same point, backs away so the third guy can try. While the third guy is trying, Critter looks like he's going to jump out of his skin if he can't get on the rock.

"Mind if I work in with you guys?" Critter asks.

I take the slight shrug to mean okay.

They don't say anything, but when the third guy falls, at the same point the other two did, he backs away and nods to Critter.

Critter steps up to the rock, chalks his hands, assesses the features. Then he grabs the first holds and is in motion. He is graceful. I remember how attractive his grace was the first time I saw him traversing around the climbing gym. Midnight Lightning is one of those impossibly reachy boulder problems, but Critter's long arms and height seem to make him glide up it. He gets to the same spot the others did and falls. But it was his first try. They have obviously been working this out for a while. They are, apparently, impressed. At least they're impressed enough to speak.

"Nice," one guy says.

"Yeah," says another.

Then, all four of them look at me.

"You want to try this, Amy?" Critter asks.

Hmm, I wonder, *does Amy want to try this?* Sure, she'll try anything. She's got no fear of what people will think because . . . well, because she doesn't actually exist.

I pull on my climbing shoes, stretch my arms, hang from my fingertips on the boulder for a few seconds.

"It's left foot here, right hand here," one of the guys says, slapping the rock to show me where.

"No beta," I snap. I hate it when guys figure that, 1) I can't work it out myself, and 2) their six-foot-four moves will work for my five-foot-three body.

They fall silent, and I can feel the three boulder boys willing me to fall early to punish me for my insolence. Critter stands behind me to spot me. Very chivalrous; I will obviously fall since only a handful of people have ever made it to the top of this boulder. And it's getting dark now, so I can barely see the holds.

The granite is smooth under my fingers. It's overhanging and bulgy. I stem out, pull myself up, reach, pull, get a foot high. God, it feels great to be on rock again. My right hand slides blindly over the stone, searching for the next hold. Is this the one that was an impossible reach?

"Lunge for it, Amy," Critter says from below me. "You can do it."

I sink my body low for a split second, then spring up, feet pushing hard, left hand yanking down. I slap the rock up high. Nothing to grasp.

I'm weightless, falling. I hit Critter's outstretched arms and we fall together onto the crash pad.

"Nice!" one of the boulder boys says. "I've never seen someone as short as you get so close to that hold."

Neither Critter nor I rush to get up out of our comfortable tangle of arms and legs. I have to admit, I liked him catching me.

"You'll get it tomorrow when you can see it better," says Critter. "You were almost there."

Finally we get up off the crash pad and brush ourselves off.

ONE HUNDRED NINE

CRITTER/HUNTER

Soft crash pad, soft girl. Why do there have to be three crag rats standing there looking at us? I do notice that P.K. seems to sink into me for a moment or two before she hops up. But one thing is for certain: I will not make any moves on her tonight. If she's still carrying around that "insane person" stigma in her head, she'll only be weirded out by me.

P.K./AMY

"Look at this." Critter points, and leads me up the hill behind Midnight Lightning so we can get a better view. Half Dome stands, a gray specter against a darkening sky.

"I can't even believe I'm *here*," I say.

"Yeah, me neither," he says. "There's so much amazing rock here you couldn't even climb it in a lifetime."

What if I really was Amy, I wonder, and he really was Hunter; artist and prelaw student, with no past of discovering "crazy person" labels? I glance at him in the waning light. Can't I just walk into that identity now, out here with the wild, powerful energy of the rocks all around us, where no one knows us, where we can be whoever we want to be? Can't I just decide to drop all the stuff from the past that made P.K. turn away from Critter, and be *new*, here and now?

Clouds open up to the moon and it makes the air go silver.

"I guess we'd better find a place to throw down our bags," Critter says.

I nod and we walk back to the tent area. There are campfires now. As we walk by the gatherings, I hear Russian, French, German, British accents. I feel like I've traveled to a foreign land.

I duck into the women's room to wash up. I look in the mirror. I don't even look like P.K. anymore. I *am* new.

When I come out, Critter is waiting for me. "I see a good spot for our bags," he says.

I follow him. *I'm Amy, he's Hunter. We are new*, I tell my-self as we walk. He stops. We're in a clearing, not too close to other tents, under tall pines and a silver moon, on soft pine needles. *We are new.* I look up at him, and before I know it, I'm reaching up, sliding my hands behind his neck, pulling him toward me. *I'm Amy, he's Hunter.* His first kiss is tenta-tive. Then we move on to the second kiss. . . .

ONE HUNDRED ELEVEN

CRITTER/HUNTER

Is this a surprise or what? At first I can't even believe it. I think maybe she wants to whisper something in my ear, or maybe she saw a tick on my neck and she's trying to get it off. But then we're kissing, and I mean *really* kissing, as in tongue and all, and I'm grabbing her, pulling her against me, and she's not pushing away.

I am aware of every movement, every texture; lips, breath, skin. Even with my eyes closed I can see her colors sparkle peach with glitter sprinkles of light. My breathing is deep and ragged, and so is hers, but we both know there is only one direction to go with this: we're in a public campground with no tent. We begin to slow down. As we slow, the mes-sage in our lips changes, from *I want you* to *I accept you, just as you are, even with everything I know about you.*

After the last soft kiss, I wrap my arms low against her back and hold her. We sway. A night bird calls out.

P.K. / AMY

The fact is, Hunter is just as good a kisser as Critter was, and Amy likes it just as much as P.K. ever did. Maybe more.

It's a long time before my pulse stops racing, a long time before we let go of each other. I try to act nonchalant as I shake out my sleeping bag and lay it on my sleeping pad next to his. It's amazing how many times I've slept *next* to this guy, with minimal body involvement. I think of the tent that's probably still in Dante's car. Probably best that we don't have it tonight.

We settle in, snug in our bags, our faces inches from each other. It's much colder here than in Red Rocks. May is still early spring in Yosemite.

"What do you want to do tomorrow?" he asks me.

At first I think he must be asking me if I want to get a hotel room or something, but then I realize he is talking about climbing. I'm glad he can't see me blush in the dark. "Something on El Cap," I say. "Something classic and challenging."

"We can link The Moratorium and East Buttress," he says. "The Moratorium is four pitches—the hardest is five-eleven-b —and then we're at the base of East Buttress, which is another thirteen pitches. The hardest pitch on East Buttress is five-ten-b, but higher up it gets easier—five-six, five-seven. We can move fast and finish well before dark."

"You sure you haven't been here before?" I ask. "You sound like you know the place."

He shakes his head. "No, but I've got parts of the guide-book pretty much memorized. I've always wanted to come here to climb."

Exhaustion makes my eyelids heavy. I want it to be morning so I can be on the rocks again, with Critter, climbing free. I get comfortable, ready to go to sleep. I yawn. "That sounds great," I say. "Good night, Hunter."

"Good night, Amy."

I fall asleep listening to the wind brush through the pine trees above us, the energy of our kisses still running through my body.

ONE HUNDRED THIRTEEN

CRITTER/HUNTER

Footsteps crunching near my head awaken me. I think, briefly, *Someone is stealing our packs.* I open my eyes and try to focus. It's early morning, already getting light. The footsteps hurry away, probably just someone going to or from the bathroom. Our packs are still there. And it's a great time to get a start on a long route.

"Amy," I whisper, and jostle her shoulder. "You ready to climb?"

She groans.

"Shhh," I say. "People are still sleeping. We want them to stay asleep so we can get a jump on The Moratorium."

It's cold. The sun isn't quite up yet. I grab the jacket Dante gave me out of my pack and put it on, cinching the hood around my face. Then I rummage in P.K.'s—I mean Amy's—pack and find her wool hat and jacket. I throw them to her. She hasn't moved yet. "Come on, girl. We're in the Valley. Don't you want to climb?"

She nods sleepily.

I take the trek to the washroom. The cold water makes me even colder, but it also makes me more awake. I'm itching, maybe even desperate, to get onto the rocks. There's way too much pent-up energy in my body. I figure if P.K. and I are going to keep things pretty innocent between us, the next best thing is to hit El Cap with all that energy and let it blast me up some heinous route.

When I come back I'm glad to see she's on her way to the washroom. I heat water on our camp stove and pour instant oatmeal and dry milk into our plastic bowls. I've got a hot breakfast waiting when she returns.

Around us, people are starting to unzip tents and make coffee. We eat fast, spurred on by the thought that everyone else in Camp Four might have their sights set on The Moratorium for today.

We dump our gear out onto a picnic table to see what we've got. We haven't climbed since Red Rocks and don't know if Dante ended up with anything essential. As we sort through the jumble of biners, slings, cams, nuts, hexes, and tricams, I feel the climbing ritual begin to calm me. Sort gear, load packs, hike, find the route, rack up, leave solid ground. I glance at P.K.'s face as she counts quickdraws, and I can see it in her, too. We are in our element.

"Looks like all Dante was carrying was the other rope, the doubles on cams, ascenders, and his personal stuff," she says. "We're golden."

"Oh good, no ascenders," I say.

P.K. struggles to make PBJs with a plastic spoon—our knife stayed with the confiscated stuff at Best Care—while I fill our CamelBaks with water from a nearby spigot. Unfortunately, our momentum gets interrupted by a clueless tourist who wanders into Camp Four.

"Man, that's a lot of stuff!" he says, eyeing the piles of gear. He's kind of tubby, wearing brand new "outdoor" clothing, and has a very loud voice. "Are you kids going climbing?"

I'm tempted to say, "No, we're leaving on a bus tour with the blue hairs." But I figure even übernerds deserve politeness, so I just say, "Yep."

"Yeah?" The guy actually sits down on the picnic table, like he's settling in for a long interview. "I want to do some climbing here, too. I've been going to the rock gym, and figure it's time to get outdoors, you know?"

We busy ourselves loading our packs. "Maybe you should hire a climbing guide," I suggest.

"Oh! Good idea," he says. Then he holds up one finger. "Excuse me, that's my cell phone. It's on vibrate." He takes his phone out of his pocket and opens it. "I'll call them back," he says. He pushes a few buttons and flips it closed again.

P.K. finishes loading her pack and is about to put it on, but Mr. Übernerd grabs it from her and hoists it clumsily. "Wow, that's heavy," he says, amazed. "I hope I don't have to carry that much stuff when I go climbing outside."

I can see P.K.'s impatience building. She puts her hand out for her pack. He gives it to her. She slings it onto her back and cinches down the straps. "Come on, Hunter, we've got to go now."

But our friend is not ready to leave. "So, if I hire a guide, which climb should I do?" he asks.

"What Does The Inside of Your Nose Smell Like," P.K. says.

The guy looks at her, confused. He puts his hand up to his nose, and, remarkably, has nothing to say.

"It's a five-four, great for beginners," P.K. says. "Also, I'm So Embarrassed For You."

The guy shakes his head. "Why?" he asks.

"Because it's a five-seven and I thought you might like something a little more challenging," P.K. says.

We have been quickly backing away, extricating ourselves.

"Oh, I get it," the guy says, laughing. "Those are names of climbs!"

"Yep," says P.K. "You also might like Women and Money."

The guy looks confused for a moment, but then catches on, and by now we are safely on our way.

"Bye, be careful," he calls to us.

Before we're even totally out of earshot, I burst out laughing. "How did you make up those ridiculous route titles so fast?" I ask.

"I didn't," she says. "But do you think he'll be upset if he finds out they're at Joshua Tree and not here?"

I stop laughing. "You mean those are actual climbs?"

"Yeah. Daria and I used to go through the J. Tree guide-book just to look at the route names. They're *insane*," she says. Then her face clouds. "Uh, sorry. I mean they're . . . outrageous."

It takes me a minute to realize she's apologizing for her use of the word *insane*. It's suddenly awkward between us, silent. I feel the labels creeping back. Humor—that fixes everything.

"Yeah, I guess technically a route name can't be insane. Only people can," I say.

I seem to have miscalculated the humor potential of insanity. The silence deepens. There's only the *crunch, crunch* of our feet on the trail.

That's it. I'm fed up. I grab her arm, swing her around to face me, then I pull her to me and kiss her. She thoroughly kisses me back. When we're done, I look straight into her eyes. "I didn't want you to get confused again," I say.

"I'm not," she promises.

We resume hiking, and every time I glance at her she's doing the I'm-trying-not-to-grin-but-I'm-grinning-anyway thing.

ONE HUNDRED FOURTEEN

P.K.

This is the happiest I've ever been. And we haven't even started climbing yet. What an amazing life this would be: I could do homeschooling and get three credits of philosophy for listening to Critter's wild ideas about life, three credits of "life skills" for navigating the world of bus travel, camping, and survival, and eighteen credits of phys ed for hiking and climbing. Maybe one credit of "consumer math" for making our money last. Critter and I could travel from one climbing area to the next doing classic routes or putting up new ones. One credit of history for learning about the first ascents, and geology credits for studying the rock formations. I'd never go back to those dead, boring classrooms. Daria and I would start college at the same time with our homeschool high school diplomas. Critter would go to a college nearby and we'd visit each other on weekends. . . .

"Hmm. Nice colors," Critter says. "You thinking about the climb or *what*?" He grins at me. He obviously thinks he has caught me fantasizing about him.

"Yes, I'm thinking about climbing," I say coyly. No need for him to know he was part of the fantasy.

We come upon two guys stopped on the trail, consulting a guidebook. Critter asks them if we can take a look at it.

"*Sì, sì*, yes," the guys say.

It turns out they're from Italy, on an extended climbing trip to the States. We talk for a few minutes, them in broken English, us with our hands as much as possible. Critter turns to The Moratorium and East Buttress in the guidebook. He wants me to see the routes, laid out with each pitch drawn and photographed. And he wants to refresh his memory of both the climbs and the hike to them.

Once we get our bearings we say "*Grazie*" and "*Ciao*" to

the guys, and we're on our way. Soon, above the tall pines, we see El Cap looming. It looks like something dropped from the moon: huge, sculpted gray walls leading to a blunt summit. It makes me dizzy to look up at it. It's as if, when the earth was being created, someone said, "We need a playground for rock climbers," and, *splat*, this thing dropped from the sky.

We scramble up a talus field and find our line on the cliff: to the right of a buttress, above a large blocky boulder, an obvious seam that continues up as far as we can see. I lay both my palms against the rock. Smooth, cold granite. I look at Critter.

"Oh, *yeah*," he says, grinning. "Ladies first?"

I crane my neck, looking up. "This first pitch is five-ten-d, to a bolted belay, right?" I ask, trying to remember what I saw in the guidebook.

"Yep," he says.

This will be a piece of cake compared to climbing off into the unknown in Red Rocks and building our own belay stations. I begin to rack up, and my brain calms. I stop planning my future, stop wondering if Critter and I will still be together by the time we start college. My focus narrows: choose the gear, clip it on, tie into the rope. We stuff everything we might need into our CamelBaks: PBJs, energy bars, rolled-up jackets, headlamps. And we clip our hiking shoes onto the back of our harnesses so we can give our feet a break from tight climbing shoes on the descent. We leave our backpacks at the base of the climb.

Soon I'm ready to leave the ground, and then there are no thoughts at all. Just the rock, and me defying gravity.

ONE HUNDRED FIFTEEN

CRITTER

Belaying a girl on the first pitch: the best view of her butt you could ever hope for. And she's kicking it up there, too—slapping in gear and gliding up like she's taking a walk.

"Oh my God," she calls down. "It's like this crack was *created* for gear! It's so easy to get great placements."

"You're looking hot up there," I call to her.

She shoots me a mock disapproving look.

"As a climber," I say. "You're climbing *hot*."

She shakes her head, smiling, and places another piece of gear. I shoot out rope as she clips. I'm looking forward to the tiny belay ledge.

ONE HUNDRED SIXTEEN

P.K.

I never knew that quite so much reaching around, leaning in close, and grabbing of your climbing partner's body parts was necessary on a small belay ledge. We switch the gear from my harness to Critter's, and he takes off on the next pitch.

ONE HUNDRED SEVENTEEN

CRITTER

Made the most of the ledge, and now it's time for me to expend some serious energy on the rocks. My lead is 5.10b to 5.10d, and if I keep going I can take on the thin, tricky 5.11b section as well. P.K. will probably be safer tonight if I wear myself out a bit on that 5.11b part.

ONE HUNDRED EIGHTEEN

P.K.

As soon as Critter takes off, I start wondering what's going to happen at the top of this climb. Three more pitches and we'll be on a huge ledge with *privacy.* The energy between us is so thick even I can almost see the color of it: red for *hot.* I'm a little scared. I've never felt anything this strong before, never had my body in such a war with my common sense.

ONE HUNDRED NINETEEN

CRITTER

P.K. was right, the crack eats gear like it was chiseled with nuts and cams in mind. The climbing is consistently hard, an endurance fest. I feel the balance in my body, pulling and pushing at angles just right to move me up. Cranking hard on sun-drenched rock—just what I needed to put some of the fire out.

ONE HUNDRED TWENTY

P. K.

He's doing the sexy Russian-ballet-dancer thing again—grace in motion. He's at the crux, the 5.11b section. The wind has picked up and it's blowing the rope around. That can't be helpful on that thin crack. *Come on, Critter, you can do it.* He's above his gear maybe five feet, his toes in the crack, doing finger locks. He pops. I lock off the belay, feel the jolt. He dangles, rubbing his forearms.

"You want this?" he calls down. "You're the five-eleven-thin leader. And there's a great belay stance just below it."

At that moment I love him—for offering me the lead, for believing I can do it every bit as well as, maybe better than, he can. The wind is picking up. I look behind me. Dark clouds are amassing far in the distance. Are they heading this way? I don't *need* the 11b section, I decide. I'm having enough fun as it is.

"Nah, you take it," I say. "You'll get it."

Rested, he starts back up. He moves past his last piece, places a piece above his head, and grunts his way up that hard section. He lets out a victory yell and I know he's above it.

CRITTER

Hanging belay. It's definitely not the most comfortable way to go, given the fact that my harness is digging into my flesh, but it's my only choice. My feet brace against the wall. I pull up the rope, draping it in loops over one thigh, and call to P.K. that she's on belay. I have to shout loudly, as the wind whips my voice away.

P.K. cruises the crack. It's thin, just the right size for her small hands.

"Nice job," I say as she joins me. I clove-hitch her rope into the belay, and then she, too, gets to hang in her harness and feel it biting into her flesh.

"What do you think about this wind?" she asks. "And those black clouds are closer than they were."

I survey the sky. It seems as if we can see the entire state of California from here, so it's no wonder we can see some black clouds among the white puffy ones and the sections of bright blue sky. "They might blow past," I say. "When we get to the top of The Moratorium we can decide. We'll either take the scramble down, or if it looks clear, we can start up East Buttress."

She agrees and we start switching gear to her harness. She's having trouble keeping her feet against the wall—the wind keeps blowing her off balance. I spread my legs around her and stabilize her in front of me.

"This is just to protect you," I say.

"Oh, *thank* you," she says sarcastically, but I can tell she doesn't mind.

The wind gusts again. I wrap my arms around her and nuzzle the back of her neck.

"Critter, stop," she objects. "Don't distract me. I'm about to *lead*."

She's right. I keep a professional distance of about one inch.

ONE HUNDRED TWENTY-TWO

P.K.

This boy is driving me crazy. And now we're almost to that big ledge. My next pitch is 5.8, which would be a pleasant, fun cruise with no wind. As it is, the rope is being blown off to the side and it pulls on me like a moving thirty-pound weight, threatening to pitch me off. I zero in, focus on the rock in front of me. Cool gray granite, nice and grippy for my feet, chunky holds for my hands, just a bit of an overhang. One move at a time, slot a piece, and on to the next move. I try to forget about the boy below me, the big private ledge above me, and the tangled wind all around me.

ONE HUNDRED TWENTY-THREE

CRITTER

P.K. has no trouble at all with the third pitch. Thank God she goes fast. I am more than ready to get out of the hanging belay.

When I join her at her belay ledge we both have to admit that the black clouds are bigger and may, in fact, be coming our way. Wearing lots of metal on an exposed cliff face during an electrical storm is not highly recommended, so we plan to be ready to bail from the top of The Moratorium if we have to. Too bad. The top, on that big ledge, is where I thought we might have some fun.

ONE HUNDRED TWENTY-FOUR

P.K.

Critter starts up his lead. He tells me to stay huddled close to the rock face in case he dislodges anything. The guidebook says this last pitch is loose. My heart is pounding. Is it because of the wind and the black clouds swirling toward us? The fear of rockfall? Or is it because of what could happen—what part of me wants to happen—a hundred feet above me on that ledge?

ONE HUNDRED TWENTY-FIVE

CRITTER

I finish the pitch and survey the ledge. It's got a few trees for shade, some bushes for privacy, an amazing, romantic view of the valley, and some nice flat rock that's plenty wide enough for two teenagers to lie down on. I belay P.K. up. When she gets to the top, her face is flushed. I clip her into the anchor to make her safe. Then I offer her a drink from my CamelBak. As she leans in close, I unclip her helmet. My helmet is already off. The wind whips our short hair, tugs at our clothes. As soon as P.K. finishes drinking, I kiss her. There is a crack of thunder in the distance, a bolt of lightning on the horizon. We talk in between kisses, our mouths close together.

"Critter, there's no time . . . got to get down . . . the storm."

"There *is* time . . . the storm is far away."

I lean her back, cradle her head in one hand, let my other hand wander. . . .

ONE HUNDRED TWENTY-SIX

P.K.

I'm on my back, Critter is half on top of me. I am *wanting*, and scared. His hand goes under my shirt, touches the skin of my back, slides toward my belly. I stiffen. He feels it, retreats to my back again, traces my spine. It sends shivers all through me. I sink deeper into it, losing myself.

Suddenly, it's as if an alarm goes off. *What if this gets out of control?* And in that instant, I remember: our harnesses. They're as good as chastity belts. I nearly laugh with relief. I kiss Critter more deeply and lie back and let the pleasure wash over me.

ONE HUNDRED TWENTY-SEVEN

CRITTER

Stupid harness. Note to self: the only thing more uncomfortable than a hanging belay in a tight harness is making out in a tight harness. There just isn't *space.* I've got to chill this out before I'm in severe pain, but I don't want her to think I'm not interested. The wind is dying back, so I can't even use the storm as an excuse. I hear voices down below. Saved. We have another one of those mouth-to-mouth between-kisses conversations.

"P.K. there's people coming . . . better stop."

"They're way below . . . we've got time."

"They might want East Buttress . . . we should start up."

"Not *yet.*"

And then we're not mouth to mouth anymore. I'm pulled back, looking at her in earnest. "East Buttress is thirteen pitches. What if they're faster climbers than we are? What if they're hiking up here along the descent scramble? They'll be here in no time. I don't want them crowding us or trying to pass us or any of that."

ONE HUNDRED TWENTY-EIGHT

P. K.

It's a myth that guys are more interested in sex than anything else. It's sports they're most interested in, plain and simple.

I get up, brush myself off, put my helmet back on. I guess at least I'm not having to beat him away with a stick like some guys I've dated. I really should appreciate him for that.

We scan the sky. The dark clouds move off in the distance, and it's sunny, warm, still breezy but not violently windy anymore. Perfect climbing weather. "So we start up the thirteen pitches and hope for no more storms?" I ask.

"I'm game if you are," he says.

We scramble up a steep fourth-class section to a nice belay ledge below the start of East Buttress. I look up. The first pitch is a chimney, and it's my lead.

"The chimney is five-nine, and you'll get a beautiful crack above it," Critter says.

As I worm and stem my way up the narrow chimney, I hear more voices down below. It sounds like an entire climbing school is amassing at the base of The Moratorium. I'm glad we got here early.

Critter is right: once I squirm my way out of the chimney, I'm rewarded with a beautiful crack system with great gear.

Once I get high enough, I can see the people down below. There are at least fifteen of them.

I bring Critter up to the belay ledge and point down. "I'm glad we didn't get behind that conga line," I say.

He squints as he peers down. "Does it look to you like they're wearing uniforms? Like it's police or something?"

It looks like he could be right. "Maybe," I say.

Worry crosses his face.

"It's probably just park police doing some training thing," I say. "Or maybe someone fell. Or maybe there's been a drug bust. I heard these guys talking in the campground and they said there's a *jail* right here in the Valley, mostly because of all the people who bring drugs in."

He still looks a bit worried, so I start handing him gear. That brings him back to the moment. "The next pitch is a five-ten-a crack to a five-nine arête, but then we'll be cruising on five-six and five-seven for a while," he says.

As I belay him, I've got time to study the group below. They've got binoculars. Maybe they're just tourists who wanted a steep hike.

Critter is almost to the arête now, moving quickly and gracefully. That's when we hear it, broadcast from a loud-speaker down below. "Critter Bellarico and P.K. Aubrey, come down off the wall. Mr. Bellarico, you are under arrest."

ONE HUNDRED TWENTY-NINE

CRITTER

So this is where it ends.

And we didn't even get to do East Buttress.

"Critter, oh my God!" P.K. cries.

"Lower me," I tell her. I down-climb to my last piece, then weight the rope and let P.K. bring me down.

"What do we do now?" she says. Her eyes are wide with fear.

I huddle close to her on the ledge. "We do what they say and go down," I tell her. "They'll deliver you to your father, and take me to the nearest hospital with a psych ward. It's what we knew would happen all along. It's just happening sooner than we hoped, that's all."

"But what are they arresting you for?" she asks. "You didn't do anything wrong."

I shrug. "It's *the* cops," I say simply. "It's what they do if you leave the mental ward when you're diagnosed psychotic."

She leans over the side. "Well, what are they going to do if we *don't* come down?" she asks. "Come up here and get us?"

Is she suggesting what I think she's suggesting?

She raises one eyebrow at me. "You want to climb this thing?"

"Heck yeah, but are you sure? It can only get you in more trouble with your parents," I say.

She scoffs. "Who cares? We're in the Valley, on a great climb. Why make it easy for them?"

I look up at the vast cliff above, beckoning to us. We've come all the way here. They can damn well arrest me *after* we do the route.

"Belay is on," P.K. says firmly.

"Climbing," I say.

"Climb on."

ONE HUNDRED THIRTY

P.K.

Now I understand why there aren't any other climbers around; the police must have set up a blockade somewhere. Well, more rock for us.

Critter gets back on the wall and moves up. I can't help grinning. This is such a perfect you-can't-make-me situation. They must be scratching their heads down there.

They start in again with that ridiculous loudspeaker. "This is the police. Critter Bellarico, come down off the wall immediately. You are officially a fugitive from the law. P.K. Aubrey, a rescue team is on its way up to get you."

That's curious. A rescue team for me, handcuffs for him? Critter seems to be unfazed by the ranting from down below. He climbs smoothly, making the 5.9 arête look easy.

"Mr. Bellarico, we know you escaped from the Mount Olivet Hospital and that you're off your medications and not thinking straight. Come down and no one will get hurt."

Would they shut up already? This has got to be rattling Critter. "You're looking good, Critter," I call to him. "They can't stop us, okay?"

He doesn't say anything, but his legs start into sewing-machine shakes, and I know they're getting to him.

"Mr. Bellarico, this is your final warning. Descend immediately."

Critter is reaching above his head, placing a cam. He slots it, takes a quickdraw off his harness, clips it in. As he reaches down for the rope, I hear it: gunshot. And Critter's body drops off the wall.

ONE HUNDRED THIRTY-ONE

CRITTER

"Critter!" she screams, and keeps on screaming until I wave my arms to prove to her I'm not dead. The blast startled me and made me slip, that's all.

P.K. lowers me down to the belay ledge quickly. "Oh, God, Critter, are you all right?"

I feel my arms, my legs, my shoulders. I'm not hit, just shell-shocked. "I'm fine," I say. I sit close to her on the ledge. They won't shoot at me if I'm with her.

"This is crazy," she says. "Why would they want to *kill* you?"

Why would they want to kill me? They're coming after P.K. with a rescue team and coming after me with guns. . . . It starts to coalesce in my mind. "I'm officially a danger to myself and others," I say. "They think I'm unstable. Maybe they think I'll try to take you with me in a suicide scheme, like we're going to climb up to the top and jump off. Your dad knows you're with me and believes you're in mortal danger, so maybe he has engineered this huge P.K.-rescue mission. And I'm the bad guy."

P.K. rubs her forehead. "I think you might be right," she says.

"Let's go down," I say, resigned to the inevitable.

She shakes her head. "No way," she says. "Police do crazy things to teenagers—shoot them and then say the kid pulled a gun first, and then it turns out all the kid had was a cell phone but now he's dead so it doesn't matter. What if we rappel down like they want us to, and you reach for your chalk bag or water or something? They can shoot you and say it was in self-defense. I'm not going down for them, Critter."

I blink at her, not even sure I'm understanding her correctly. "So . . . you want to go *up*?" I ask.

We both look at the cliff rising above us.

"Can we lose them if we can get to the top?" she asks.

I picture the top, remembering what I've heard about it. "There are all kinds of ways down. There's a rappel and scramble descent, a steep hike that leads right to Camp Four, even an easy eight-mile trail to Tamarack Flat. It's big up there, lots of forest and trails. I think we *could* lose them. We could even hide out overnight and hike out tomorrow."

She frowns a bit. "If we could just stay close together . . ."

"Right," I say. "They sure don't want to shoot *you*."

She looks at me, her eyes suddenly bright, and says one word: "Simulclimb!"

ONE HUNDRED THIRTY-TWO

P.K.

It's risky, but it's the only way. And it's less risky than facing those trigger-happy cops down there.

Critter unties and we pull the rope, then he reties into his end.

"We'll keep about forty feet of rope between us," Critter says.

"Forty feet? I don't want you so far from me," I object.

"They'd never risk the shot, not from so far away," he says.

"Thirty," I insist.

We each coil nearly half the rope to sling over a shoulder. Once we've fed out about thirty feet from the middle of the rope, we each clip into a figure-eight knot tied on a bight.

We'll be climbing at the same time. If one of us falls, the other's body weight will be the belay.

We move in tandem, the rope outstretched between us. Critter uses the gear he placed before and places more gear so that we've always got several pieces of protection between us. He clips the rope in, and I unclip and take the pieces out as I reach them.

Critter looks so exposed, his back like a target. I'm shaking. My hands are sweaty and keep slipping in the crack no matter how much chalk I use.

"So far, so good, huh?" I say, trying to sound calm.

"Yep," he says.

We keep moving, silently. The wind swishes past the rocks. I strain my ears, dreading another gunshot blast.

ONE HUNDRED THIRTY-THREE

CRITTER

Nothing like a gun at your back to hurtle you into the present moment.

There is no one shooting at me *now.*

There are no bullet holes in my body *now.*

Now I am on the rock.

The sun is on my back, the wind brushes my skin.

P.K. is just below me.

She is safe.

I am safe.

When I reach the next belay ledge, I haul myself over the edge and dive behind some bushes for protection. I clip myself to a tree and belay P.K. up the last few feet.

She is pale and shaky. *What are you doing to her?* the

hamster demands. *For God's sake, turn yourself in and let her save herself. This is way too risky.*

"P.K.," I begin. "We can go down. I—"

"*No*, Critter. I got you into this mess, and I am *not* going to let you get killed because of me." She glares at me, her jaw set.

Inwardly I raise one eyebrow to the hamster. *You want to argue with that?* I ask him. For once, he has nothing to say.

"Okay, then let's outrun them," I say. "I'll lead since I remember the route from the guidebook. This next part is easy, five-six and five-seven, and we can fly if we place less gear. We'll try to keep two pieces between us, but just make sure there's always at least one piece in the rock, okay?"

She nods.

"Every piece I put in will be solid, trust me," I say.

"I trust you," she says quickly.

"But P.K., sometimes we'll be depending on one piece to hold a fall. It'll be best not to fall."

"It's easy rock. I won't fall. Neither will you," she says confidently.

"Then let's get something to eat and drink now. We're going to outrun the bullets *and* the rescue team."

I take a few bites of an energy bar. P.K. says her stomach is in knots, so she just drinks water. We get the rope and gear in place.

"Ready?" I ask.

"Ready," she says.

P.K.

We start out moving among bushes and trees. It's a fourth-class scramble and I feel protected by the undergrowth. But then we get to the rock face again and we are exposed.

The police are yelling at us through that loudspeaker again, but I shut them out. We move in a rhythm. Each time I reach a piece of gear, I look up to make sure another piece is already clipped. Then I take it out and keep moving. I try to stay closer to Critter than thirty feet. I feel like his body-guard.

The climbing is easy, an arête with large, blocky holds. Critter is moving quickly, calmly. We come to a set of bolts; it's the belay station. But we move right past it, not stopping.

We do another scramble through bushes and scree. We stop just long enough for me to give Critter back the gear I have taken out of the rock, take a few swigs of water and a pee break, and then start moving again.

I hear voices way below us. "Belay is on." "Climbing." "Climb on." Is it the "rescue" team? They'll never catch us climbing *that* way, I think with satisfaction.

The next pitch is an easy crack. I actually find myself en-joying the climbing. The rocks are sun-drenched and invit-ing. We haven't heard any more gunshots. The "rescue" team is stopping to belay, so they're not even an issue. I've been so focused, there has been no room in my thoughts for fear. I feel *good*. Critter has been silent. I wonder if he is all right.

"Critter, you doing okay?" I ask.

"Excellent," he says.

A whole host of Critterisms come to mind. We are safe. There is never anything to be afraid of. Life is one hundred percent adventure.

"Are you scared?" I ask him, just to test him a bit.

He places a nut and yanks on it to set it. "Nope," he says.

"Yeah, it's weird. Neither am I," I say. "I'm sort of not thinking at all, just feeling good." I climb to the nut, wait as he places a hex up above, then grab my nut tool to get that set nut out.

"It's usually thinking that *makes* you scared," he says. He climbs past the hex and I move up as well.

All of a sudden it's like my brain remembers that it hasn't been nearly active enough, and it starts up with a vengeance. *What if the police start shooting again? What if the rescue team starts simulclimbing once they get to the easy part, and they catch up to you? What if they find you at the top?* But instead of believing any of it, I just laugh.

"That's what you call the hamster, right?" I ask. "The thoughts that go round and round in your head?"

"Yep." He sets another nut, clips to it, and I quickly take out the hex and move up. "I named it the hamster when I realized it wasn't actually *me*. It's more like a resident tormenter." He pulls a cam off his rack, places it, clips the rope in, moves up.

"Ha. A resident tormenter. That's exactly what my mind feels like sometimes," I say. "So I can decide not to buy into it?" I move up to the cam, take it out of the rock, clip it to my harness.

"Right," he says. "As soon as you take a step back, you're free."

That's when I see it—what I've done. I've taken out the cam and Critter hasn't placed another piece yet. We are clinging to a thin, vertical crack, seven hundred feet above the valley floor, with no protection whatsoever. I freeze, unable to move.

"Critter, I messed up," I cry. "Put a piece in!" I grip the rock hard.

He looks down. His eyes widen. "Hang on, P.K. Don't panic. And don't think about it."

I start to hyperventilate. I go dizzy. If I fall I'll pull both of us to our deaths. *Don't think about it.* I try to calm my breathing. I rest my helmet against the rock. *Whatever you do, don't look down.*

I hear the snap of a biner above me. "Okay," Critter says. "You can peek now."

I look up and he is grinning. The nice fat number-three cam is placed in front of him.

"Oh. My. God," I say. "I'm so sorry. I got distracted talking."

"No worries," he says cheerfully. "It woke me up. Did it wake you up?"

I nod slowly. Every one of my cells is awake with adrenaline.

"You ready to keep going?" he asks.

I shake my arms out one at a time and move my cramped fingers. "I'm ready," I say.

"That's the whole idea," Critter says, almost to himself, as he moves higher on the rock. "Waking up."

ONE HUNDRED THIRTY-FIVE

CRITTER

After the little no-protection-an-eighth-of-a-mile-in-the-air incident, we've both got adrenaline speed. I can hear the voices of two climbers way below us and figure they're the guys the police have sent up to save P.K. from me. I doubt they can catch us, even if they start simulclimbing once they're past the hard pitches.

We come to a ledge and I realize we're already at the base of the two 5.9 pitches. We'll need more protection here. We're both tired, adrenaline-shot, hungry, and dehydrated. In this state, either of us could fall on a 5.9. We stop for P.K. to give me gear, and I start to lengthen the rope between us.

"What are you doing?" she demands.

"We need two or three pieces of gear in the rock now. This is five-nine," I say.

She scoffs. "You think we're going to fall on five-nine?"

I knew she was going to argue. She wants to protect me by staying close. I want to protect her with extra gear. I continue lengthening the rope.

"Critter, I don't want you so far from me," she says firmly.

"Look down," I say. We can still see the tight knot of police gathered below—waiting for the rescue team to bring P.K. down, I assume. But they are way below us now—we have definitely gained some height. "They won't try shooting from that far away even if we're a little farther apart. Trust me on this."

"All right," she says grudgingly.

P.K.

It's hard to wait for Critter to put in a third piece before I'm allowed to take one out. But I'm glad to have the extra gear in. My muscles feel shaky. It's been too long since I've eaten anything.

We stop in an alcove to exchange gear, and I drink some water. My mind feels fuzzy. Exhaustion is setting in.

We start up the next pitch, an off-width crack that makes me contort my body in strange ways just to stay on the rock. My limbs feel heavy. And even with two or three pieces of gear between us, I don't want to fall.

"Critter, I'm losing it," I say. "I think I needed to eat more today."

"I'll stop at the next ledge and belay you up," he says. "We're almost done with the five-nine section."

When I reach him, he takes one look at me and shakes his head. "Your colors are washed out like you're about to faint," he says.

I flop down on the ledge and lean back against a tree.

"It's a clear case of glycogen depletion," he says, rummaging through his CamelBak pouches.

"A case of *what*?" I mumble.

"Aha!" He holds up a plastic tubelike thing. "Swallow this and you'll be fine." He hesitates a moment. "If it doesn't make you throw up."

He tears it open and hands it to me. It's a tube of goo. Sweet, weird-tasting pink goo. But I'll try anything, so I suck it down. It's like eating sugary ectoplasm. I wash it down with water.

"Better?" he asks, bright-eyed.

I groan. But I do feel slightly more awake. It must have been caffeinated ectoplasm.

"How about a sandwich?" he asks, offering me his PBJ.

I shake my head. "Too heavy. That *will* make me throw up."

"Four more easy pitches and we'll be up there," he assures me. "It's five-five to five-seven now."

I drink some more water. "I can do it," I say.

ONE HUNDRED THIRTY-SEVEN

CRITTER

They'll catch up with you soon, says the hamster.

Sooner or later, I know, I answer.

No, soon, the hamster insists.

We're on the 5.7 pitch. Even on this easy rock my arms feel shaky. It has been a long, high-adrenaline day.

P.K. starts talking, and I'm glad because she drowns out the hamster. "So, there's forest at the top, right?" she asks.

"Right."

"Do you think we should rap and scramble off, or hike out, or what?" she asks.

I've calculated it in my head already. "I figure they're probably hiking in on the easy trail from Tamarack Flat, so we shouldn't take that trail out, at least not today. Or they might be taking the steep trail from the Valley. Both hikes are eight miles long, so we've got plenty of time before any of those out-of-shape police get here. If we take the rap and scramble descent, then we're just in the Valley again, and they'll have an easier time finding us."

"Critter, you said we could lose them easy. Now I've climbed up over a thousand feet, and you're telling me there's no way out?" Her voice is tight with frustration. She's too tired for the long explanation. I should have just given her the quick and dirty solution.

"No, of course there's a way out," I say. "We get up to the top, chill out for a while, eat our sandwiches. I haven't heard the rescue dudes for a while so I figure they're so far down we'll have at least an hour to kill. Then we hike around and find a nice gulley to rap into. We rap far enough down that no one can see us, find a comfy place, and settle in for the evening. The police get there, search the area, figure we're gone, and leave. We spend the night somewhere up there. In the morning we hike to Tamarack Flat and continue with our excellent adventure."

"Good," she says. "I'm glad we don't have to hike out tonight."

As soon as P.K. stops talking, the hamster starts up again. *You'll be back in the mental hospital soon*, it says.

I know that. Sooner or later, I say.

No, soon, it tells me.

P.K.

Thank God the climbing is easier from here on. I couldn't do another hard pitch right now if my life depended on it.

Critter's plan sounds good. Especially the part about chilling out and finding a safe place to sleep before we have to do any more physical exertion.

The route is vertical face with knobby holds. I'm exhausted, barely paying attention, just wanting to get to the top. I reach for a hold, grasp it, and pull. Suddenly I'm weightless, falling, and the hold—a fist-sized rock—is flying free from my hand, dropping.

"Rock!" I shout—the warning to anyone below to press themselves against the cliff. Falling rocks kill.

"Rock! Rock!" Critter shouts. He has fallen, too, pulled off the cliff by my body weight.

Then we hear it, like an echo: "Rock! Rock!" Our warning cry being passed on. But the voices are so close! They're maybe only a hundred feet down. How did they do it? Have they been simulclimbing in silence?

"Oh my God, they're right behind us!" I cry.

Critter and I dangle near each other. "Okay, it's okay," he says, but he's clearly flustered. "Can you get back on the rock?"

I get back on and hold tight while he climbs above me.

"We can move fast," he says. "Don't worry. We can still beat them. We can still lose them up there."

Cold sweat runs down my back. My whole body trembles. I fell on an easy 5.7. Can I even make it to the top?

ONE HUNDRED THIRTY-NINE

CRITTER

Did P.K.'s dad hire some kind of stealth SWAT team? He's got money, and he's desperate to get his daughter back. I wouldn't put anything past him. And if those guys on our tail believe I'm armed and dangerous, I wouldn't put anything past them, either.

They could hurt you, the hamster says.

I know, I say.

They could hurt you bad.

I know! I snap.

They could hurt her, too . . . accidentally, on purpose.

Shut up! Shut up shut up shut up!

I shove the hamster away and watch him fall fifteen hundred feet. Then I dive inside myself. I bring my awareness to my hands and arms, reaching, pulling; to my feet and legs, stepping, pushing. I spread my awareness to my whole body, this shell that houses my spirit. Then I expand, stretch beyond my body, feel how *I*, the real me, am so much more than this small body on a cliff. I remember how the real me was feeling terrific, hanging with my grandpa, during those brief minutes when my body was, technically, dead. And I feel safe. I know *I* am safe.

"Critter, *hurry*," P.K.'s voice comes, urgent, panicked. "They're right below us."

I don't think. I *act*.

I place two big nuts, clip a sling between them, then put my foot into the sling and jump on it. Those are a couple of terminally set nuts.

"P.K., don't take out those two nuts. Just unclip and climb past," I tell her.

The rock backs off, gets easier. I can see the scramble ahead of us, a hiking trail that will lead to the top of the formation.

I get behind a big boulder, brace my feet, and give P.K. a hip belay. She comes up over the edge. Her eyes are wild.

"They've got a radio. They said—" she begins.

But there's no time for words. No time to assure her that who she really is, is safe. Only time for one word.

"Run!"

ONE HUNDRED FORTY

P.K.

We're on mud and scree, running past low bushes. My feet ache in my climbing shoes. Critter uses the rope between us to pull me along. I trip, go sprawling, bash my knee on a sharp rock. I cry out. But there's the rope, pulling me up, helping me forward, letting me know I won't be left behind.

We're on a wide slope, going up and left. This must lead to the top. I glance behind us. No one there yet.

The words I heard over the radio echo in my mind: *I don't care what you do to subdue the boy.* And the climber's answer: *Right. That'll be fun. We've almost got them.*

The slope levels out a bit, opens up. There are a few tall pines, boulders, exposed roots on the well-worn trail. This is where we were supposed to eat and rest. We keep running.

Suddenly Critter stops. He ducks behind a boulder. I fall to my knees and creep up behind him. "What is it?" I whisper frantically.

"Police. With dogs. I just barely caught a glimpse—I don't think they saw us. But how did they get here already?"

It doesn't matter how they got here so fast. They did, and they're here.

He looks at me, his eyes gentle. "P.K., do you want to just walk out there now? Give ourselves up? It's not that bad. You'll go back to your family and I'll go back to the hospital. We always knew it would end that way, right?"

I shake my head. *I don't care what you do to subdue the boy.* "I don't trust them, Critter," I say. "I'm afraid of what they'll do to you. They think you're a criminal—a kidnapper or something. You said we could lose them, now let's *do* it."

He smiles, gets that familiar twinkle in his eyes. "All right, then turn around. I'm taking a quick pee break."

I huff and turn around. "Can't you hold it, Critter? We need to run!"

It's the fastest pee break in history, and we're off and running again, keeping low, stumbling over scree and tangles of roots. We're noisy, the gear on our harnesses clanging. The rope still connects us. I follow Critter as he weaves around trees. Then I see them in the corner of my vision—the "rescue" climbers coming from the cliff, running.

ONE HUNDRED FORTY-ONE

CRITTER

I see flashes of color through the trees. They're coming fast.

The only way out is down.

I veer off the trail. I plunge through the thick underbrush, the setting sun glaring in my eyes. Up ahead I see where the trees end at, the sheer cliff edge. We break out into the open.

Behind us I can hear them, crashing through the undergrowth, talking into their radios, coming closer. A tall pine stands at the edge. I run to it and stop. Far below is the valley, laid out in greens and grays. Below me is sheer cliff all the way to the valley floor. I hear P.K.'s ragged breathing beside me.

"You ready to lose them?" I ask.

She looks at me, confused.

I take her shoulders and move her to the right of the tree. I stand to the left of it. "On three, we jump," I say. "Ready?"

She nods, but I can see the panic rising in her eyes and in her colors.

"Don't think about it," I say quickly. The voices are closer. "One, two, *three!*"

ONE HUNDRED FORTY-TWO

P.K.

On *three* I leap.

If Critter doesn't jump, my body weight will pull us both down over a thousand feet, to death.

I fly free.

ONE HUNDRED FORTY-THREE

CRITTER

On *three* I don't move.

P.K. jumps.

ONE HUNDRED FORTY-FOUR

P.K.

Where is the end of this rope? Didn't he *jump*?

And then it happens. My body is flying free, and my mind and spirit follow. For the flash of a second I know I could be anywhere, endure anything, and still be amazingly, intensely happy. I *am* free.

The rope pulls taut and I bounce against the wall with a thud. I swing a bit, and look up to see Critter dangling well above me. How did he get way up there?

I find holds on the rock and climb, giving him slack so he slides down closer to me. "Why are you so far above me?" I ask.

"I jumped after I made sure you did," he says. "If I jumped and you chickened out . . ."

I shudder. "Yeah, duh—we'd be on our way to the valley floor about now."

He nods. Then he's all action. "Quick. I want to pull the rope. The dogs will sniff it out easy. Let's swing over there."

To our left is a huge diagonal roof. If we can swing under it, we'll be well hidden from above. We push ourselves along the rock and grab holds to pull ourselves up under the roof. Then we quickly place gear and clip directly to it. I untie from my end of the rope. As Critter yanks the rope down, I coil it in big loops, and in seconds we've got it down and safe. Then we wait, silent, hanging under the roof.

Voices. They're rummaging around up there, radioing each other. We catch snatches of the conversations. ". . . thought I saw them . . . must have . . ." I hear a dog whine. "Yeah, he smells something . . . no one here."

Then I hear it, very loud and metallic, coming through the radio. It chills me—the voice, the cadence, the accent, the urgency. They are all so familiar and it is like cold water in my bones. "Damn it all, how could you get so close and *lose* them? I'm coming up there. I'll search all night if I have to."

Critter looks at me. "Wow," he whispers. "That cop is taking his job seriously, huh?"

My lips are trembling. I don't want to cry. My throat is tight and painful. "That wasn't a cop," I whisper. I wipe tears from my cheeks. "That was my father."

ONE HUNDRED FORTY-FIVE

CRITTER

I wrap my arms around her, as best I can with both of us hanging on gear. The voices and footsteps move away from the cliff edge.

"It's just—" She tries to talk, but her voice sounds strangled by tears that want to come.

I give her a squeeze. "It's okay," I say. I think I understand. If she's feeling the same thing I'm feeling, then I do understand.

"I wish I could just"—she takes a deep, shuddery breath—"go home."

Her tears have got me choked up now, too. "Exactly," I say. "It's like they make this plan that's supposed to be good for you, and they say it's because they love you and want the best for you. And then they send you away."

She pulls back and looks at me with teary eyes. "That's exactly it," she says. "Don't get me wrong, Critter; I've loved climbing with you. It's just I wish we could go climb for a few days, without being chased, and then go *home*. My brothers will be back from college for the summer soon, and I really miss them." She blinks and wipes tears away quickly. "I even miss my stupid parents."

"Yep," I say. "I wish I could go back to my own room in my own house. I'd play gin rummy with my little sister, go running with my dad. I'd even do yard work with my mom without complaining."

She gives me a sad smile. "And we could go climbing on weekends?"

"Absolutely," I say.

She sniffles and wipes her nose with her T-shirt. The sun is lower now, and it's getting chilly. The voices from up above have disappeared.

"We're going to be here awhile. Let's get a little more comfortable," I suggest.

The roof above us has a matching slanting platform below it, which forms a big, diagonal chimney of sorts. We add more gear to our life station and lengthen our tethers so we can move around better. We take off our tight rock shoes and change into our hiking shoes. We take the extra gear off our harnesses and hang it on a sling, along with our helmets, rock shoes, and CamelBaks. I coil the rope properly so it's ready for us to climb out of here when we figure the "rescuers" are gone.

We can kind of sit on the steeply sloping wall of the chimney. It's not very comfortable, but it beats hanging.

"I need to take a pee break," I say.

"Again?" she asks.

"That last one was a mini—for the dogs, to give them

something to interest them and give us more time to get away," I say.

She laughs, and turns her back to give me privacy.

When I'm done, I see she has made herself a temporary chest harness out of slings so she can lower her hip harness to pee. "My turn," she says, and we switch places. "I just hope there's no one climbing below us."

We get as comfortable as we can on the slope of the chimney, eat our PBJs, and drink most of our remaining water.

"Those set nuts, were those to buy us time, too?" P.K. asks.

"Yep," I say. "I figured no climber can pass up booty. I've known guys who would hang there banging away at a stuck nut in lightning and pouring rain just to get a free piece of gear."

The sun sets and the temperature drops quickly. We put our jackets on, but soon P.K. is rubbing her hands to try to keep warm.

I put the coiled rope behind me and sit back against it, against the rock, wedged into the corner. "Come here," I say, and pull P.K. to sit in front of me. I wrap my legs and arms around her, a human blanket. "Better?" I ask.

She relaxes into me. "Yes." She clasps her arms over mine. "We're sleeping here?"

"Yes, I'm sorry, all the campgrounds and hotel rooms are full tonight," I say.

"I just hope we're not overpaying for this," she says.

There are wispy clouds in the sky and they're lit up orange, pink, and silver with the afterglow of the sunset. We watch in silence as the colors change and the sky goes from clear blue to indigo.

"Critter, " P.K. says after a while, "what you said before about you going back to the hospital. You don't belong there. Can't you explain that to your parents? They don't have to send you back, do they?"

I shrug. "I tried everything to convince them I didn't belong there. They're too scared to believe me. So I've just always known I'd end up there again."

She sits forward and turns to look at me. "What happened to all your stuff about imagining what you want and your thoughts will bring it to you? Huh? Critter, you made *clouds* disappear. Parents should be easy after that."

I can't help smiling, because she remembered. Then I shake my head. "But you can't change *people*," I say. "It's okay, though." I try to sound upbeat. "All I have to do is accept it and I'll be fine. It's only resistance that causes suffering."

She scowls at me. "Bull," she says. "I don't mean bull about that you'll be fine. I mean bull that you can't change them. You should at least *try*." She turns forward again, settles back against me. "Imagine it perfect."

Bats swoop by us, making their high-pitched squeals.

"Go ahead," she says. "Imagine it perfect. Tell me."

"Oh, man," I say. "Let's see . . . I go back to live at home, in my own room. Or maybe we move back to upstate New York near the Gunks with all my old friends? No, then I wouldn't ever see you. So, um, I go back to school . . . but I *hated* that new school." I sigh, frustrated.

"Maybe that's your problem," she says. "You can't imagine it good because you don't know what you want. So you can only imagine what you had before."

I tickle her. "When did you get so wise?" I ask, as she elbows me in the ribs.

"Hanging out with you."

The bats squeal by again.

"Do you think those bats are looking for hair?" she asks.

"They won't find much here," I say.

P.K. yawns. "Tell you what, if you can't do it, I'll imagine it perfect for you." She gets comfy. I take it this is going to be involved. "You go back to living at home because your parents now totally understand and respect you. Amazingly, the school district lines get redrawn over the summer, and you get to go to my high school instead of your lousy school."

"But I thought you hated your high school, too," I interrupt her. "And aren't you going to be a homeschooler?"

"Shush," she says. "We're changing your life right now, not mine." She is quiet a moment. "Okay, over the summer my high school principal announces there will be no more standardized tests, so the teachers can use all sorts of creative ways to teach us important stuff, instead of just getting us ready for tests, so my high school is no longer boring and pointless. And it's also much better because you and I are in some of the same classes."

"Okay, sounds good," I say.

"Our parents are absolutely cool about us traveling together," she continues, "so we take road trips on weekends and holidays to different climbing areas—oh, I forgot, your parents also give you a car."

I laugh.

"Stop laughing," she says. "This is important. What kind of car do you want?"

"Um—a Jeep."

"Okay, so we take your Jeep on road trips." She yawns again. "Anything else you want?" she asks.

I lean in and kiss her on the cheek. "Nope. I think you've got it all figured out."

It's dark now. And we are both plenty weary enough to fall asleep on a slanted, cold rock.

ONE HUNDRED FORTY-SIX

P.K.

I awaken and don't know where I am. Then it all floods back: the climb, the gunshots, being chased, jumping. The moon is up now, peeking in and out of clouds. I feel Critter's body behind me, his chest rising and falling in sleep. I'm cramped and cold, and my mouth is dry as sandpaper.

I also remember my father's voice. *I'm coming up there. I'll search all night if I have to.* I wonder what time it is, where he was when he said that, and if he is here yet, at the top, just above us. I listen for footsteps, voices, anything. Nothing but the night.

I watch the moon, lighting the clouds when it is behind

them, then its sharp, clear light as it slides out from a cloud and hangs alone in the inky sky. In again: fuzzy, muted light; out again: crystal clear. I am mesmerized by the magic of it. I shift a little, trying to get more comfortable on the hard rock. Critter shifts, too, and sighs in his sleep. A question comes to me, as if floating on an updraft: *What would you do if you weren't afraid?* And the answer comes, too, sharp and crystal clear as the moonlight: *I would leave. Now.*

ONE HUNDRED FORTY-SEVEN

CRITTER

"Critter, wake up."

She is jostling me, poking me. It is still deep night, with a bright moon. My sleepy brain sifts through all the reasons she might need me to wake up, and finds no answers. "What's up?" I ask. It's intensely uncomfortable on this cold rock. I'd rather have stayed asleep.

"I need to go," she says. "I need to climb out of here. And you need to stay. I can see it—it's the only way."

Now I'm wide-awake. I can feel grief dig two fingers into my heart and press. P.K. sounds very sure about this. It is not going to be easy. "Explain?" I say. I'd like to at least understand.

She curls sideways against me and lays her head on my chest. I wrap my arms tight around her.

"If I climb out I might be able to find my dad, or the cops, or someone. I'll turn myself in and go with them. But you stay *here*." She presses one hand against my heart. "I'll tell them you're long gone. I'll say you're on your way to San Francisco, that they should search for you in Golden Gate Park if they want to find you." She sits up and looks at me. "Then you go free. Don't let them put you back in that place." She lies against me and I hold her. I run my hand through her hair, along her cheek and the line of her chin, touch her lips. She kisses my fingers.

Now. She is here now.

ONE HUNDRED FORTY-EIGHT

P.K.

"I'll . . . rack up," I say.

I start clipping gear onto my harness. I can't stand to drag this out, this saying good-bye. And there will be no kissing good-bye, because my mouth is dry, my teeth are fuzzy, and I'm sure my breath smells like something crawled up in there and died.

Critter is flaking out the rope. He is so silent, so not like himself.

"You okay?" I ask.

"Uh . . . actually, I'm in the early stages of grief and loss, so I'm not so good," he says.

I shake my head slightly. "I'm going to see you again, right? You can come back home after your parents change their minds. When they see that you've been fine with no meds for weeks, or months, don't you think they'll let you come back home?"

We are in silver moonlight, but Critter's face is in shadow, so I can't see his expression. He doesn't answer my question, just keeps flaking out the rope to get it ready for me.

Now I've got a lump in my throat. But I *have* to leave. If I stay, they'll eventually catch us both, and he'll be locked up again. If I go, my dad will end the search, and Critter will have some breathing room—hopefully enough so that he can disappear for a while.

"Critter, it's the only way," I say.

"I know it is," he says.

Good. At least he understands.

"You want me to secure the rope at the top so you can get out when you're ready?" I ask.

"No," he says. "Even if you hide it, the dogs will find it. Throw it back down to me. I'll self-belay my way out."

I put on my rock shoes. When I go to tighten the laces, one of them snaps. I curse, but Critter calmly takes the broken lace from me, puts my foot in his lap, relaces the shoe, and ties it for me.

"Thanks," I say. Then, suddenly I realize this is our last chance to make plans. "Hey, can you memorize my cell number? Or my e-mail?" I ask.

He shakes his head.

"Why *not*?" What could be so hard about a little memorization?

"Because if I contact you, it puts too much pressure on

you. If they know you're in touch with me, they'll hound you to find out where I am."

What, then? "All right, you know my last name, and I live on Cherry Avenue—that's just south of the city. Come find me when you get back."

"Sounds like a plan," he says. Then he takes a deep breath. "Back to the moment. You're here now, and you're about to climb, so it's all good, right?" he says.

"All good," I say. "And I'd *better* see you again because you'll have some of my gear, and I want it back."

He hands me the end of the rope so I can tie in. "I'll mail it to you," he says. But the old humor and spark is back in his voice.

I cock my head to the side, and give him a sultry look. "No, I want *personal* delivery," I say.

He grins.

"And I want a chance to kiss you again when there is less fuzz on my teeth," I tell him.

"Definitely," he says.

We purse our lips and give each other a closed-mouth, morning-breath kiss. Then he grabs me and pulls me close, and we hold each other for a long moment. "Okay," he says finally. "Time to concentrate."

I'll be leading out of here on unknown rock of unknown difficulty, in the dark. I try to focus my mind. I put my headlamp on and grab all my stuff: CamelBak, hiking shoes, helmet. While Critter isn't looking, I cram my extra cash into a pocket of his CamelBak. He'll need it more than I will.

"We'd better use rope signals so we stay quiet," Critter says. "Three hard pulls means you're off belay, okay?"

"Got it," I say.

"You can do this," he says. He must have sensed my nervousness about the unknown rock in the dark.

I take a deep breath. "On belay?"

"Belay on."

"Climbing."

"Climb on."

I hesitate. "Critter?"

"Yes."

"Imagine it perfect, okay? For both of us."

ONE HUNDRED FORTY-NINE

CRITTER

She climbs up and over the lip of the chimney, and the light from her headlamp fades. I hear her gear clanking as she moves. I feed out rope. She stops, and I hear the light scrape of gear in the crack, then the snap of a biner, and I know she's clipped into a piece. The rope lengthens between us as she moves farther from me. Then, finally, I feel the three hard tugs. She's at the top. A few moments later, her end of the rope comes slicing through the air, and I know she's gone.

I must now be in the second stage of grief and loss, where the girl actually leaves and the cliff on which you're spending the night feels very cold and dark and lonely.

ONE HUNDRED FIFTY

P.K.

Thank God the climb is easy. Or maybe it just seems easy because all I can see of it is what is in front of me in the beam of my headlamp. Critter would probably say that's what being in the present moment is like—paying attention only to what is right in front of you.

At the top, I untie. I hold on to the rope an extra moment. It's the last link between Critter and me. Then I let it drop and hear it swoosh down. "Come find me soon," I whisper.

I sit on a rock and change into my hiking shoes. A shadow moves and it startles me. But it's just the branches of trees swaying in the moonlight. It's quiet, with only the night sounds of wind in the pines and an owl hooting far away. I don't even know what direction to go in. *Just don't fall off the cliff*, I tell myself, and I start walking.

A memory comes to me, of myself when I was about four years old, wandering through the crowds at an amusement park, crying. I'd lost my dad and didn't think I'd ever find him. I feel like that lost child now.

ONE HUNDRED FIFTY-ONE

CRITTER

It's so cold without P.K.'s body heat to warm me. I curl up in a ball and try to sleep.

Imagine it perfect.

Right now, a blanket would be nice.

ONE HUNDRED FIFTY-TWO

P.K.

I see a flicker of light. A fire? A flashlight? Whatever it is, there's a *person* out there. I rush toward the light, stumble over a rock, pick myself up, and keep going. I will it to flash again. There it is, to my left. No voices, but definitely a light. I remind myself I don't need to be afraid now. It was Critter they wanted to hurt, not me. I'm making plenty of noise, breaking sticks as I go, the gear on my harness clanging. Suddenly the light comes on and, bam, it's in my eyes and I'm blinded. I hold up my arms and turn my head away. The light swoops down, away from me. I look up. There's a figure—a man. He's holding a flashlight pointed at the ground. *Oh, God*, I think, *if it's an ax murderer I'm screwed.* I don't move. The man with the light comes toward me slowly. I hope that rather than an ax murderer, he's actually a lost tourist from Iowa who could possibly lead us both out of here with that flashlight.

Then I hear it, cutting through the forest quiet with all the familiarity of home: "P.K.?"

I run to him, and I'm the lost child again—miraculously, impossibly, finding her father, and crying with relief.

ONE HUNDRED FIFTY-THREE

CRITTER

Dawn. As usual, it's perfect.

Yes, I'm sore and cramped, incredibly thirsty and way hungry. I'm heartbroken and lonely and cold.

But I'm also free. And the day, and therefore the adventure, is just beginning.

ONE HUNDRED FIFTY-FOUR

P.K.

Dad holds me while I cry. He cries, too, which is way out of character and *really* disconcerting. It makes me feel rotten for having put them through so much.

He gives me water, which I gulp down desperately, and a strawberry yogurt, which tastes like food for a god. The rest of the rescue team went back down for the night, but he stayed—just in case he could find me. He radios them to tell them there's no need to come back up in the daylight—I'm safe. I am thankful for him. Solid, dependable, sometimes unreasonable Dad.

The eastern sky has begun to glow, and we can just barely see the path. He knows the way back to Tamarack Flat. We've got eight miles to hike and talk.

ONE HUNDRED FIFTY-FIVE
CRITTER

I sniff the air. Could it be? I sniff again. *Definitely.* Coffee. There are bivouackers close by, on one of the long El Cap routes. They'll be climbing soon, hopefully coming my way.

I'll be a chameleon. I'll climb out at the same time as the coffee people finish their route. I'll hang with them as we hike out. I'll blend in, looking like a typical climber dude. No one will guess I'm Yosemite Valley's number-one most-wanted criminal. And hopefully no one will notice that I just had my heart ripped out.

ONE HUNDRED FIFTY-SIX
P.K.

As soon as we get cell service, we call Mom. Turns out she is my advocate. I don't even have to threaten to run away again if they send me to boarding school because she has told Dad to bring me home and she's not letting me out of her sight. It'll make traveling to climb a little tough, but it's way better than boarding school.

Dad and I talk. The sun comes up and warms us as we walk. The trail is easy, and we pass other hikers. We are a father and daughter out for a day together—and changing our relationship in fundamental ways. He listens. I am honest. It is real. And by the time we get to Tamarack Flat and pile into his rental car, I feel more understood than I have in a long time. I'll need to compromise, though. No homeschool. No boarding school, just regular school—and I have to promise to go to classes and get decent grades.

Dad says we have to drive to the police station to return the two-way radio they loaned him, to show them in person that he found me, and to inform them that Critter is on his way to San Francisco. I am almost too tired to keep my eyes open by the time we get there, so I just sit on a bench while Dad explains everything. I hear them apologizing to Dad about the gunshot. "Against protocol," they say, and that it was a rookie cop who thought he'd heard the order to fire. That rookie cop will be disciplined, they assure my dad.

There is an officer there who looks strangely familiar. He brings two backpacks, mine and Critter's, over to me.

"These are yours," he says. Then he leans in close so only I can hear, and says, "Those climbs are at Joshua Tree, not here, you little brat."

I glare at him, recognizing him now. I have a sneaking suspicion he's the one who told that rookie cop to fire.

"Oh, and *this*"—he holds my pack up, reaches his hand into the space between the shoulder straps and the pack's lining, and pulls something out—"is mine."

I frown, confused. It's something square and flat.

"GPS chip," he says, and slips it into his pocket.

Fortunately, at that moment my dad comes over and interrupts this lovely interaction, which saves me from being arrested for assaulting an officer.

"Ready to go, honey?" he asks.

I nod and get to my feet, eager to get out of there.

The officer reaches out to shake Dad's hand. "Mr. Aubrey, the photographs of the kids—the ones I took of them sleeping next to the backpacks to confirm their identities, and the one I took later as they were leaving to climb—they're still in my cell phone. Do you want them? If not, I'll destroy them." He smirks at me. I can tell these details are for my benefit, to show me how when I thought I was cleverly teasing him with the names of those J. Tree climbs, he was actually much more cleverly turning us in.

"No, no," my dad says. "I don't need the photos, and they're in my e-mail anyway. Please destroy them. And thank you so much for the work you did finding the kids. Good luck finding the boy."

"You're welcome, sir," he says. "And don't worry. If the boy is still somewhere in the park, we'll find him."

Run away. Run far away. Please don't let them find you, Critter.

ONE HUNDRED FIFTY-SEVEN

P.K.

On the way to the airport I lie down in the backseat to go to sleep. Something crinkles under my head and I pull out a piece of paper. It's one of those stupid flyers that was in the climbing shop in Fresno. It's got descriptions of me and Critter under our photos. And it's got descriptions of our climbing packs. Of course. Mom was the one who sewed those logos on there—all the national park logos on mine, and somehow they figured out (from someone in Las Vegas when they caught us there?) that we had Tom's old pack with the University of Vermont logo on it. No wonder that cop took photos of us that morning, sleeping next to our packs. Even with our hair changed, our packs gave us away. Then he e-mailed the photos to my dad to make sure it was really us, and the "rescue" mission got into full swing. When he came to our campsite and lifted up my pack, that must have been when he slipped the GPS chip into it. I crumple up the flyer and throw it on the floor. At least Critter won't be with those packs anymore. No doubt the police picked them up from the bottom of the climb to use as "exhibits A and B" or something.

I'm ready to shut it all out—the sadness over leaving Critter, the weirdness of going home, the wondering what it will be like. Will I feel out of place now, after all I've been through? Will my friends accept me? Will I be able to deal with school and household chores and the city after the wild freedom of the rocks? The car seat is the most comfortable thing I've lain down on in a while, so I do shut it all out and fall asleep.

P.K.

Reentry.

The good parts:

1. Being able to take a shower whenever I want to, and sleeping in my own bed.
2. Seeing my brothers again. Them wanting to hear all about the climbing and being totally impressed that I helped put in a new route.
3. Mom being thrilled that I cut my dreads off. Her taking me for a real haircut to have it styled right.
4. Daria listening to *everything* and still loving me.
5. There being only two weeks of school left, and me managing to pass all of my classes (mostly Cs) except algebra-trig, despite my "unexcused absences."

The bad parts:

1. Having "the talk" with Mom, in which she assures me that she and Dad are prepared to prosecute "that boy" in the event that, during our time together, he "did something" to me. Even though it hugely embarrasses her, I come right out and tell her what it is she

really wants to know, which is that I'm still a virgin. There is no more mention of prosecution after that.

2. The guys—Slink, Pinebox, and Adam— badgering me about running off with Critter. "That guy turned out to be crazy, right? And turns out you didn't know him? Dude, how crazy was he?" I mostly ignore them. They're just jealous, and pathetic for deciding not to come with me when I gave them all a chance to.

3. Feeling cooped up in classrooms (it's going to be a long summer of math classes) and my own house (I am *so* grounded). Sometimes, when the longing for the wild gets strong enough that I think I'll jump out of my skin, I take a ladder and climb up onto the roof for a while.

4. Missing Critter.

5. Missing Critter. Missing Critter. Missing Critter.

ONE HUNDRED FIFTY-NINE

P. K.

June is here and gone, and still no word from Critter. What did I expect? That he'd show up on my doorstep after having parked his new Jeep in our driveway? Well . . . yes.

July is hot. I finish summer school. I manage to survive the unair-conditioned classroom and algebra-trig for the second time, and pass it. We take a family vacation to the beach, and Daria comes with us. We rent surfboards and get trashed trying to stand up on them. By the end of the first week my brother Tom is getting the hang of it, but Daria, Les, and I are still getting trashed.

At night Daria and I stay up late talking and she helps me sort out some of my thoughts and feelings. What if Critter *is* back, but he's in the mental hospital again so he can't contact me? What if he's back, living at home, but he's afraid of my parents, so he doesn't dare let me know he's here? What if something happened to him and he's *not* back? By the end of the vacation I know what I have to do. I'm just not sure I have the courage to do it.

ONE HUNDRED SIXTY

P.K.

Early August. I've looked down the list of Bellaricos in the phone book so many times I think I have all five of the numbers memorized. All I have to do is call each of them and ask for Charlotte. I'm sure I remember right that that's his mother's name. When she gets on the phone, I'll say I'm a friend of Critter's and I was wondering how he's doing. It's simple. Why don't I have the guts to do it?

I wish my parents and the Bellaricos had gotten in touch with each other while they were looking for Critter and me, so that now I'd have an opening. But what were my parents going to say—"We hope you find your son, and when you do, we're going to prosecute him"? And I guess the Bellaricos are so embarrassed by Critter's "illness," and afraid that he really was planning to rope me into a dual suicide or something, they were too guilt-ridden to contact my parents. Maybe they were scared of my parents, too—scared of their anger at Critter.

Maybe he'll be home soon and come find me, I think, and I don't pick up the phone.

ONE HUNDRED SIXTY-ONE

P.K.

August is almost over. He's *got* to be back by now. I didn't give him that much cash. And how long did he think it would take his parents to change their minds about the mental hospital, anyway? They've got to be convinced by now that if he has lasted this long without drugs or counseling, and without offing himself, he is fine.

I stare at the list of Bellaricos again. It's Saturday. People will be home. *Just dial*, I tell myself. But I'm paralyzed. *What would I do if I weren't afraid?* I take a deep breath. I can almost hear Critter's voice: *Don't think about it. It's thinking that makes you scared most of the time.* I open my cell phone and dial the first number on the list.

As it rings, I grip the phone hard, listening to the rings as if that sound is the only thing that exists. "Hi, you've reached the Bellarico residence. If you'd like to leave a message for Molly, press one; for Steve, press two."

I press "end" and let out a shaky breath. One down, four to go. I dial the next number. An older man answers and says no one by the name of Charlotte lives there. I thank him and apologize for the wrong number. It's getting easier. I dial the third number and get that weird tonal message that says the number I have reached is not in service. I press "end" and stare at my phone. My stomach tightens. Could they have moved back to upstate New York without Critter even telling me? Maybe that's what he wanted when he imagined it perfect: to be back up there with all his old friends and climbing buddies, at his old school. Has he forgotten about me?

Stop thinking, I admonish myself. I'm doing the create-a-bad-scenario thing again. There are two more numbers on the list.

I dial. It rings seven or eight times. I expect an answering machine, but then I hear a woman's voice, "Hello?"

"Hi, I was calling for Charlotte Bellarico," I say.

"This is she."

I'm frozen. I can't speak.

"Hello? This is Charlotte Bellarico; may I help you?"

I will my tongue to be unstuck. "Uh . . . yes." I blurt out my practiced line. "I'm a friend of Critter's and I was calling to see how he's doing."

There is silence on the other end of the phone. Then she speaks hesitantly. "Who . . . is this?"

I didn't practice a fake name or any way to sidestep the truth. "This is P.K.," I say.

She lets her breath out in a rush. Then she asks, "Where are you, P.K.? Are you still at home? The police told us your father brought you back—we were so relieved to hear that."

"Yes, ma'am, I'm still at home," I say.

"Good," she says. "I'm sure your parents are very happy to have you there."

"Yes, they are," I say. Then I can't wait any longer. "Is Critter home, too?"

She is silent for a long moment. Then she says, "P.K., can you have your mother or father bring you over here? We have letters for you that Critter sent."

Letters! I say yes, my mom will bring me over. I get the address and look it up on the Internet. All this time they were only ten miles away? Then I pack up my gym climbing stuff like I'm heading to the rock gym. It's the only place I'm allowed to go on my own.

I tell my mom and dad I'm going to the gym and I'll be back in a few hours.

"I thought you couldn't get anyone to meet you there today," my mom says.

"Yeah. I decided to go on my own and just boulder around," I tell her.

I'm on my bike speeding down the street before she has a chance to say, "But you *never* go to the rock gym by yourself."

Critter's house is a small brick rambler in one of those neighborhoods that was total suburbs in the 1940s and now is more like part of the city. I stash my bike behind the bushes out front and walk up to the front door. *Don't think about it, just do it.* I knock.

Critter's mom is a small woman with shoulder-length brown hair and worried eyes. She looks out the door. "Will your mother come in?" she asks.

"No, she's running some errands," I lie.

She nods, as if she didn't expect my mom to want to meet her anyway.

"Come on in and sit down," she says.

Critter's dad isn't home, and neither is his sister, Jenna, but I see photos of them on an end table. His dad is tall, lanky, muscular. That's where Critter gets his build from. I also see trophies all around. Must be from the triathlons.

"Critter sent letters?" I ask. I'm not going to be very patient about getting my hands on them, I've been so desperate to have word from him.

"Yes," she says. But she doesn't go get them. "He sent letters to us, and letters to you and asked us to give them to you if you contacted us. He said not to forward them because he didn't want to make your parents angry, and didn't want the police badgering you, trying to find out where he was."

The letters have been here all this time while I've been going crazy? I keep my voice steady and polite. "Why didn't you call me to let me know they were here?" I ask. "We're the only Aubrey in the phone book."

Mrs. Bellarico looks at me as if the answer is obvious. "Be-

232 —

cause Critter is sick, sweetheart. We knew it was better for you to get back to your normal life with your friends and family, and not be reminded of the ordeal you went through with him."

Ordeal? I let my breath out in a huff. "But you're giving them to me today, right? For some reason you decided I can handle them now?" I know I'm not being very polite, but I can't help it.

"P.K.," she says, and her eyes get even more worried— worried and sad. "There's something I think you should know."

It feels like a vise grabs my chest. This cannot be good.

"Critter's father has been monitoring the police reports coming out of Yosemite—and San Francisco, too—but knowing Critter, we figured he most likely stayed where he could climb," she says. "We've been hoping they'd find him and send him home, of course. But yesterday we got a very disturbing report." She looks down at her hands in her lap. "We think they may have found him."

Finding him, that's good, right? So why does she look like it's bad news, terrible news? My breath is stuck in my throat. I wait, not wanting to hear what comes next.

"There was what appears to be a suicide at Yosemite. They found a body—" she begins.

"It's not him!" I nearly shout it. I jump to my feet. "It can't be Critter."

"Sweetheart, you do know he had suicidal tendencies," she says. Her eyes look frantic now, like she doesn't know how to calm me down.

"He *didn't* anymore," I say adamantly. "He was happy, and totally into living, and really together." My eyes blur with tears. I grind my teeth, willing myself not to cry.

"He struggled with depression," she begins again. "He very nearly died during a suicide attempt—"

"No!" I'm angry now. This is not the Critter I knew. This is who he was before his NDE or whatever he called it. His parents didn't even bother to get to know him after that. They just had him put away.

She shakes her head. She doesn't want to fight with me. "There was . . . a lot of damage. The person—a young white male—jumped, or fell, from the top of one of the highest cliffs. Critter's father is traveling out there now . . . with Critter's dental records."

I need her to stop. I'm suffocating. I have to get out of here. "I want my letters now," I say.

"I hope your parents won't mind you having them . . . now that he's . . ." Her voice trails off. She gets up and walks over to a desk. She opens a drawer and takes out a small stack of letters. I grab them from her. They are all addressed to P.K. Aubrey, c/o Bellarico. I notice the postmark of the first one. It's from Texas.

"But he's not even *in* Yosemite anymore," I say. "Look at the postmark." *You idiot, you had no right to scare me like that*, I want to say.

"Look at all the postmarks," she says. "They're from as far away as Italy and Canada. There's no way he could have traveled to each of those places. We think he was giving the letters to people he met in the park and having them mail them when they got home."

I flip through the letters, and she is right: Ohio, New Mexico, Toronto, Italia. If he wasn't having other people mail them, he must have been crisscrossing the continent, and the world, with amazing speed.

I hold the letters to my chest, like protection. "I have to go," I say.

She nods. "I just wish . . ." She speaks softly, almost more to herself than to me. "I wish we could have brought him home."

"Me too," I say quickly.

She walks me to the door and looks out. "I don't see your mother yet," she says.

"I rode my bike," I tell her, and I'm out of there.

ONE HUNDRED SIXTY-TWO

P. K.

Back at home I close myself in my bedroom and flop down on my bed with Critter's letters. They are a treasure. I go to open the first one and see that it has already been opened. His parents read this before I could. It makes me angry, but there's nothing I can do about it. And I suppose it's understandable—they thought it might help them find Critter.

I pull the letter out of the envelope and unfold it. It's cheery and upbeat—classic Critter.

Dear P.K.,

So, you met the folks!

Things are good here. Whoa—nice wad of cash you left me. Has definitely come in handy when the cheeseburger guy insists that I pay.

There are excellent people to hang with here, but no one as scintillating and wonderful as you. And so far, no cop sightings meant for me. I must be skilled at lying low.

I wonder how you're doing. I wonder a lot of things. And I miss you, P.K. I think about you every single day, every single hour.

Love,

Critter

I smile. It's as if I can feel him through his words, and he seems closer than he has in months. This letter sounds like he might be living in Golden Gate Park in San Francisco after all. And if he was thinking about me, had made some friends, and was having a great time, he would never have killed himself. A fresh wave of anger at Mrs. Bellarico sweeps over me. I hate her for scaring me so badly.

I find the next letter in the pile, in order of the postmarks, also previously opened. This is the one sent from Italy.

Dear P.K.,

Ciao bella!

That means "Hello, beautiful."

Great news—I did Il Naso! Unbelievable. I lucked

out because this guy here was ready to go, had all the
bivy stuff and aid gear, and then his partner got real
sick, so that's where I stepped in and offered to climb
it with him. It was totally incredible. We freed every-
thing up to 5.11c and aided the rest, got muscles on
our muscles from hauling the haul bags, and finished
in five days. I wish you could have been with me, P.K.
Maybe someday.

So, what's it like being back? Are you getting to
climb? Are your brothers home? I wish you could
write to me. I miss you.

Tanti baci (that means "many kisses").

Love,

Critter

Did he really go to Italy? Where else would there be a climb
called "Il Naso"? And where did all this writing in Italian
come from? I suppose he could have learned some Italian
from an Italian climbing partner. I go online to get an Italian-
English dictionary and look up "Il Naso."

Oh man. He did stay in Yosemite. And he climbed The
Nose! I do wish I'd been with him. Five days on the wall,
sleeping in a bivy sack, suspended thousands of feet above
the earth, cranking hard day after day. I would have loved
it. I sigh, swallow my jealousy, and move on to the third
letter.

Dear P.K.,

This is kind of weird, not knowing if you're getting

these or not. I told my parents not to send them to you—figured it would piss your parents off royally if you started getting letters from me. I told them to give you the letters if you came over or called, and now I'm wondering if you ever did that, or if these are just sitting in a pile someplace. I don't have any idea what your life is like now. Do you think about me anymore? Are you angry at all the trouble I got you into, with the cops and everything?

I shake my head, frowning. How could he be doubting my feelings for him? Is his memory playing tricks on him? I wish I could write to him or call him. It's frustrating not to be able to communicate. I continue reading.

> *Anyway, the climbing is still good, whenever it dries up. But it has been raining a lot lately, so there's lots of days when I just try to take cover somewhere and stay dry (still no tent).*
>
> *Are you getting to sleep in a real bed? (Stupid question.) Do you get to eat food cooked by someone other than the greasy cheeseburger guy? I know, I know— I'm still on a fabulous climbing adventure. It's just lonely sometimes.*
>
> *I hope you're doing well and that you're happy.*
> *Critter*

No "Love, Critter"? No "I miss you" or "many kisses"? I feel as though his confidence in me is slipping through my fingers, and there is nothing I can do to stop it. And the fact that his parents were right, that he does seem to be in Yosemite, is gnawing at my stomach.

I pick up the fourth letter. I notice that this one and the fifth one have not been opened, as if his parents realized they weren't learning much of anything from invading Critter's private correspondence, so they stopped doing it.

The letter is short.

> Dear P.K.,
>
> How's it going? Oh, right. You can't answer that.
>
> You know the phrase "too much of a good thing"? Well, I think I'm on the verge of having had enough great climbing.
>
> Don't know what I'll do from here. Money running out . . . thinking maybe a career as a male model should be my next move.
>
> Later,
>
> Critter

"Later"? Give me a break. *Oh, Critter, I wish I could write you back.*

I'm almost afraid to open the last letter. With his exuberance waning, his money running out, and his confidence in me totally crumbling, could he have gotten to a place of despair? Enough despair to leap off the top of El Cap? I tear the letter open slowly and start to read.

Dear P.K.,

I've decided I can't do this anymore.

It's too hard to keep writing to you, not knowing whether you still care about me.

It's too hard to keep living here. As you may have guessed, I never did leave Yosemite. (Did you decipher my code name for The Nose?) I hid out in the backcountry for a while, did the whole pick-berries/go-hungry/befriend-a-fisherman-because-he-is-an-excellent-food-source thing. When I went back to Camp 4 I shaved my head in case there were any missing-person flyers still around, but by then it was full-on summer and the police were so busy with a gazillion tourists getting into trouble with BASE jumping, drugs, and bears, they must have forgotten about looking for me.

Anyway, now everyone is leaving Camp 4, going back to school. I can't stay here—there won't even be anyone to climb with.

And it's too hard to keep scrounging for food and shelter (more rain lately, and it's also starting to get cold some nights).

So this is it. I'm done. It's over.

This is my last letter.

I've decided August 23 is the date.

I throw down the letter, lie across my bed, and sob.

P.K.

Mom hears me and rushes upstairs. She comes into my room without knocking.

"P.K., what on earth happened?" She sits down on my bed and rubs my back.

I can't talk. I can't tell her. She'd never understand. She and Dad think of Critter as "that crazy boy" who should have been locked up again.

"Call Daria," I say between sobs. "Tell Daria to come over."

Mom leaves without another word. Ever since I was eight years old I've been talking to Daria when I can't talk to my parents, so they're used to it.

I'm still weeping when Daria gets here. I've tried rereading Critter's earlier letters, to remind me of his joy and enthusiasm. But it only makes it worse. That's what I'll miss most about him.

I tell Daria the whole thing, starting with the trip to Critter's house and the awful news from his mother. She holds me and smoothes my hair. I drip tears and snot on the shoulder of her shirt.

"Oh, P.K., I'm so sorry," she says.

I cry until I'm shivery cold. Daria tries to warm my hands between hers, but it doesn't work. "Come on, get under the covers," she says. "I'm getting you some tea."

I burrow under the covers, propped up against pillows, and Daria brings me a steamy mug of tea from downstairs. I look at her with swollen eyes. "I'm glad I still have you," I say.

"Yeah, you're stuck with me," she says. "And with Adam and Slink and Pinebox—we're all still your friends. And someday you'll meet someone and have an actual boyfriend again. But right now you're allowed to cry your eyes out because this totally and completely sucks."

I let out a shuddery breath and sip my tea.

"Can I read his letters?" Daria asks.

"Yeah," I say. "Read them in order. The first ones are better."

Daria sits on the floor next to my bed to read. About the first one, she says, "Aaaw, that's so sweet." For the second one she asks, "Do you know where he was? What's that climb, Il Naso?" When I tell her, she says, "He did The Nose? Lucky dog." On the third one, she says, "Yeah, I can see how he's kind of losing confidence here." When she gets to the fourth one, she laughs at the line about the male model, but she also shakes her head and says, "Hmm."

As she reads the fifth letter she is very quiet. I close my eyes and feel the tears start up again as I remember his despairing words: *I can't do this anymore. . . . It's too hard. . . . I'm done. . . . This is my last letter.*

Then Daria says, "P.K., you are an absolute, total moron."

P. K.

"What?" I open my eyes and blink.

"You're a moron. You didn't even read this letter. You stopped after the first page. Did it even occur to you—hello?— to turn the page *over*?" She slaps the letter over on her lap. "Like *this*?" She looks at me, her eyes bugged out for emphasis. "And then read the *rest* of it?"

I grab for the letter, spilling tea on my bed. She hops up, holding the letter away from me.

"No," she says. "I don't even trust you to read it properly. Just *sit* there and listen." She points at me like she's ordering her dog to stay. I don't move.

"Let's see, *It's too hard. . . .* blah, blah, blah . . . *I'm done. It's over. . . . last letter*, yada yada, *August 23 is the date.* Then you turn the page over. *I'll start hitchhiking back then. Give me five days to get there. I need to see you, even if it means getting caught and sent back to the hospital. How about we meet for a date? Eight p.m., behind the Dumpster at the climbing gym, for old times' sake. That'll just be our meeting place, not where I'll take you for a date, of course. I should have at least thirteen cents left by then. Can't wait to see you. Please come, even if it's just to tell me you've forgotten all about me.*

Hoping for the best,
Imagining it perfect,
Critter

P.K.

Daria and I are squealing, jumping on my bed, hugging, laughing.

"Oh my God!" I cry.

Mom comes rushing up the steps. "Is this *good* squealing, I hope?" she asks.

"Yes. Very good squealing," Daria tells her.

She leaves, shaking her head. It's often best that parents don't get let in on every detail.

"Okay, so five days from the twenty-third." Daria counts on her fingers. She looks at my wall calendar. "Uh, P.K."

"Yeah?" I can't stop grinning.

"That's today. As in tonight. As in, you have a Saturday-night date with the love of your life and you've been in here blubbering instead."

My face falls. I rush to the bathroom. Daria is right behind me. We both stare into the mirror. I look terrible.

"Stupid *hamster*!" I cry, and kick the bathtub.

"What?" Daria asks, confused.

"It's just—" I bury my face in my hands. "My stupid mind created the whole scary-scenario thing out of thin air. Okay, with a little help from Critter's mom's hamster, but none of it was real *ever*. It was just a really bad story my brain made up." I stare into the mirror. "And now I look awful because of it."

"I still don't get the hamster part," Daria says.

"Never mind," I say. "I need makeup—fast."

I wash my face with cold water and blot my eyes dry. I'm not very good at putting on makeup, since I hardly ever do it, so Daria helps me. "Just a little," she says. "He likes the way you look without it."

Concealer and mascara work wonders. I blow my nose one more time. "What should I wear?" I ask, suddenly panicked again.

"Duh, whatever you normally wear to the rock gym. Your parents won't let you out of the house otherwise."

"Oh, right," I say.

I'm already wearing the right stuff, my favorite pants to climb in and a T-shirt. I don't want to take the time to change anyway. It's seven thirty. What if he's already there, waiting for me?

We announce to my parents that we're taking our bikes to the rock gym. My dad gets up out of his chair.

"Two workouts in one day, huh, P.K.?" he asks.

"Yeah," I say hesitantly. It feels like something is up.

"Well, I'll drive you, and pick you up," he announces, as if he's afraid we might argue with him.

I breathe a sigh of relief. If he suspects that one of my outings today is not actually to the rock gym, I'm glad he has picked this outing to drive me to. "That's great, Dad. We'd love a ride," I say, honestly.

"Yeah, thanks, Mr. Aubrey," Daria says.

He eyes us a little suspiciously. "I'll pick you up at ten thirty," he says.

"Eleven?" I plead. "It's Saturday."

"All right. Eleven. But no later."

He probably thinks he has outwitted us and prevented our attendance at some wild no-parental-supervision party. Not a problem.

On the way over, Daria calls each of the guys. Slink and Adam say they can meet us at the gym, and she leaves a message for Pinebox. Good. Daria will have them to climb with while I am otherwise occupied.

ONE HUNDRED SIXTY-SIX

P. K .

My dad drops us off and watches until we go into the gym. Just inside the door, I stop. I'm ready to jump out of my skin. "Drive *away*, Dad," I say under my breath.

"Give him a minute," Daria says calmly. "If he's suspicious, he's liable to wait out there awhile to see if we come out. Let's go climb."

I give her a pleading look, but she's right. I let her lead me past the check-in guys to the cave—a bouldering area with a low roof covered with holds.

"Let's boulder a bit," Daria says.

She changes into her rock shoes, but I just grab a couple of holds and start doing pull-ups. It feels good to burn a little nervous energy.

"Done," I say after ten pull-ups. "I'm going out there."

"Check for your dad's car first," Daria cautions.

"Yep," I say.

I head toward the door, and suddenly I'm scared. I haven't seen him in so long. My mind starts up. *What if he has changed? What if I'm different? What if it's not the same between us?*

I peek out the door. My dad's car is gone. I close the door again. *Well, was it ever the same from one day to the next? No. Sure, we're both different now, so it probably won't be exactly the same, but that doesn't mean it won't be good.*

I swing open the door and walk into the parking lot.

What if he doesn't show up? What if he changed his mind? What if he met some gorgeous girl on his way back? Or what if he really is the one who jumped off that cliff?

I stop and look the hamster square in the eye. *Listen, you've messed up my day enough already. Starting this second, I'm ignoring you.*

I feel the warm night breeze and look up at the few stars in the city sky. I take a deep breath. Ah, the Dumpster—what a romantic meeting place. I walk to it, blinking my eyes, trying to see someone standing there.

ONE HUNDRED SIXTY-SEVEN

P.K.

There is no one at the Dumpster.

I walk around it, in case he's behind it, even look inside (stupid me).

The hamster doesn't have to say a word.

P.K.

I see Daria walking toward me and realize I must have sat here for hours on the filthy asphalt next to the Dumpster.

"P.K." She looks around, then back at me. "Did he . . . leave already?"

I shake my head. I have no more tears, no more words.

Daria sits down next to me and huddles close. "He didn't show up," she says softly.

I hug my knees and rock a bit. I've been through it all, these past couple hours. All the places he could be, everything that could have happened or not happened, around and around on that stupid wheel.

"You know"—Daria tries to be encouraging and cheerful—"it might take him *six* days to get back instead of five."

I nod and uncurl myself to stand. I help Daria to her feet.

"We can come back tomorrow," she says.

"Okay," I say.

I feel strangely quiet inside. It's as if my emotions have had enough and are taking a hiatus.

We go inside the gym to wait for my dad. Slink, Adam, and Pinebox are all there, and the minute they see my face they want to know what happened.

"He never got here," Daria tells them.

"He stood you up. Dump him," says Adam.

"You don't need him, P.K. You've got us," says Slink.

Pinebox gives me a hug.

"*Maybe* there was *traffic*," Daria says.

P. K.

Daria promises that we'll go every day to the rock gym to keep checking. But each time we go and he's not there, I am crushed again. After three more days I can sense even Daria's confidence is wavering.

As for me, I spend my time going round and round on the wheel. I'm surprised other people can't hear it squeaking. *Maybe Critter got caught. Could he be in jail? But for what crime? Maybe he's back in the hospital, drugged up the way he said they drugged that girl Maria after she escaped. Or what if he got picked up by an ax-murderer trucker? Or was in an accident? Or maybe he stopped off at some greasy truck-stop diner on his way back and a really cute waitress saw him and hit on him and he's living with her now. Or he's home with his parents and they won't let him see me. Or maybe he found a great climbing partner who wanted to do more big walls, so he's staying in Yosemite for a couple more weeks and then he'll be back. Or he stopped off in Eldo on his way back. Or he could be the guy they found at the bottom of the cliff. . . .* I can see why they call those things exercise wheels. It all makes me tired.

I tell Daria I can't keep checking for him every day and getting hit with the disappointment over and over. She seems relieved, and we stop going to the gym.

It's time for me to fulfill my promise to my parents anyway, to do my summer reading before school starts next week. That's when a strange thing happens. I actually learn something from my schoolwork.

It's *Hamlet* by William Shakespeare. I take it out to the hammock. I figure if it's too boring, I'll just lie back and see if I'm any good at zapping clouds.

So, I'm reading, and it's not bad—kind of poetic and a good story. I get to a section where Hamlet is talking to Rosencrantz:

> HAMLET. Denmark's a prison.
>
> ROSENCRANTZ. Then is the world one.
>
> HAMLET. A goodly one, in which there are many confines, wards, and dungeons, Denmark being one o' the worst.
>
> ROSENCRANTZ. We think not so, my lord.
>
> HAMLET. Why, then 'tis none to you; for there is nothing either good or bad, but thinking makes it so: to me it is a prison.

"There is nothing either good or bad, but thinking makes it so. To me it is a prison."

So Hamlet's *thinking* makes it a prison. And Rosencrantz's thinking makes it not a prison.

I lie back in the hammock and look up at the clouds. My thinking—aka the hamster—has been making my life feel like a prison. A scary prison, with dungeons of worry and fear. And yet, it's all very simple: Critter will come back, or he won't. No amount of thinking or worrying will change that. And either way, my life will go on. My life, which is not a prison. I don't even have to go to boarding school next week.

I remember what Critter always said about all worry and fear being about the future, which doesn't even exist. Only *now* exists. So, what is *now*, I wonder? I focus on what is around me. I feel the hammock cradling me, swinging slightly. A breeze brushes my skin. It ruffles the leaves on the tree limbs above me. I see glints of gold and red among the green leaves—the first colors of fall. A bird lets out a string of notes that fade into silence. I smile as I feel something I haven't felt in a long time: joy.

ONE HUNDRED SEVENTY

P. K.

Daria comes over. I know she's checking on me, and it's sweet. I read her the passage from *Hamlet* and tell her about trying to focus on *now* instead of my fears about the future. She tells me about a fantasy novel she read this summer—*The Island*, by Aldous Huxley—where the people on this island teach a bunch of wild birds to squawk, "Attention here and now! Attention here and now!" to remind them to stay in the present moment.

"I am *so* trading in my hamster for one of those birds!" I say.

Daria laughs and shakes her head.

I start practicing "attention here and now" as I go through

my day, and I notice something amazing: it shuts the hamster right up. It's easy, too. All I have to do is pay attention to what is in front of me at any given moment and *be there*. It's just like climbing, only I start doing it even with simple things, like eating a bowl of cereal: listen to the crunch, taste the sweetness, enjoy the calories; or washing my hands: feel the warm water, smell the scent of the soap, feel the life in my body as I stand at the sink. It's like I'm finally *living* my life instead of always trying to *solve* it. *Live the adventure*, Critter would say.

Little by little, the worries and what-ifs about Critter begin to fade away. I still wonder about him, of course. But when I think of him, I try to send him this one good thought: that I still care very much about him. Whether he is still on the road, or back in the hospital, or being flown home from Yosemite in a coffin, I hope he can read my thoughts from afar the way he used to when we were together. *Critter, I love you.*

ONE HUNDRED SEVENTY-ONE

P.K.

After a couple of days off, Daria and I decide to meet at the rock gym in the evening—just to climb. We call the guys to let them know we'll be there.

I ride my bike over and do the in-the-moment thing as I go: setting sun turning red in the late summer haze; crickets and cicadas filling the air with their banter; my legs strong against my bike pedals; knowing I've got friends waiting for me at the rock gym; breeze blowing my short hair.

It's getting dark as I park my bike, lock it up, and walk inside. I love the smell of chalk dust and ropes. I say hi to the check-in guys (they just nod at gym members, since they know us), but something catches my eye. It's on the cash register, draped over the top. A shoelace. *My* shoelace. The lavender one with the orange tape on it. The one that broke off in my hand in Yosemite. The one Critter took from me before he retied my shoe. I stop, staring, my mouth open. I point wordlessly at the shoelace.

The bandanna/earring check-in guy, who I think is named Ryan, sees me and says, "Oh, yeah, somebody left that for you, P.K."

Before I can find my voice to ask who left it, the hamster starts in with full force. *It was his father who left it. He found it in Critter's pocket on his dead body with a note that said—*

"Shut up!" I shake my head hard.

"Whoa, we're testy today, huh?" the bandanna/earring/Ryan guy says, and I realize I just spoke out loud to the hamster. My face turns bright red.

"Uh, no, I wasn't talking to you, I was . . . Anyway, sorry. And thanks." I grab the shoelace, stuff it into my pocket, and march toward the cave, where I can see Daria and Pinebox warming up.

"Hey," I say.

"Hey, P.K.," Pinebox says, his voice strained from the effort of holding himself on the roof of the cave.

Daria drops onto the mat, takes one look at me, and says, "What happened now?"

I drag her off to the side where no one can hear us. I show her the shoelace, tell her the whole story, ask her what I should do. But even as I'm talking, I *know* what I should do. "I've got to go," I say, and leave her standing there looking somewhat dumbfounded.

I walk out into the night. It's cooler now—one of those late-summer evenings that hints of fall. My heart is pounding in my ears. I walk toward the Dumpster.

ONE HUNDRED SEVENTY-TWO

P.K.

There is someone sitting on the ground. He unfolds himself and stands. My breath catches in my throat. It's like I'm seeing an apparition. He's taller—definitely taller. His hair is shaggy and all blond again. I'm almost afraid to touch him, as if that might make him disappear. But he takes care of that. He grabs me and lifts me up in a bear hug. He does not disappear.

When he sets me down, I pull back to look at him, but before I can get a good look, his lips are on mine, and I'm sinking into kisses that are electric and familiar and brand-new.

CRITTER

Count down off the imagine-it-perfect list:

1. Get message to girl that even though I was
   late, I made it.

Check.

(Who knew that the trucker who promised to bring me all the way back would have a delivery in Podunk, Tennessee, break down there, and end up waiting five days for the parts to arrive?)

2. Meet girl at Dumpster.

Check.

3. Sweep girl off her feet with three months
   of pent-up I-want-to-be-with-you energy, all
   poured into a glorious make-out session.

Check.

4. Actually, I'm creating this list as I go along.

We'll know what number four is when we get to that point in the adventure.

ACKNOWLEDGMENTS

I want to thank the many people who helped me gather the information for this book: Tony Barnes, climbing guide extraordinaire, who knew about the uncharted cliffs in Red Rocks, answered my questions almost daily during the first draft, and read a final draft for accuracy. Anne Fields, who went with me on my second trip to Red Rocks and Las Vegas, where we climbed and double checked research together, and where she read an early draft in our tent at night by head lamp. Diane Kearns of Seneca Rocks Climbing School, who helped with both the big picture and the detail editing. Thanks also to Eric Owen for that first trip to Red Rocks where we did the long routes, and to Tom Thomas and Rob Borotkanics for that first trip to Yosemite where I took the long fall.

There are also myriad people who either read the manuscript to check for accuracy and give input, or shared their expertise and helped me with information about things like: life in the psych ward, escaping from mental hospitals and the legal ramifications, the nature of police work in risky situations, safe houses for runaway kids and what they can and cannot do, what the top of East Buttress looks like, and how to jumar. Some, but not all of them, are listed here: Jeff Fields, Katherine Kearns, Vernon and JoAnn Patterson, Sarah Patterson, and Claudia Putnam.

I also want to thank my editor, Tracy Gates, for encouraging me to write a book about rock climbers, and for her guidance all the way through. And many thanks to my family:

my husband Jim, for both editorial input and encouragement; my daughter Rachel, always a first reader and confidence builder; and my son Daniel, the best tour guide ever of San Francisco, including Hippie Hill—the beat goes on!